FREDDY FINAL QUEST

BOOK FIVE

IN THE GOLDEN

HAMSTER SAGA

BY Dietlof Reiche

TRANSLATED FROM THE GERMAN BY John Brownjohn

ILLUSTRATED BY Joe Cepeda

SCHOLASTIC INC.

NEW YORK   TORONTO   LONDON   AUCKLAND   SYDNEY

MEXICO CITY   NEW DELHI   HONG KONG   BUENOS AIRES

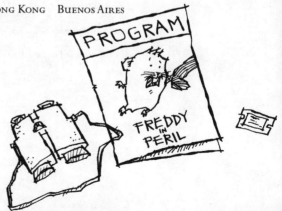

This book was originally published in hardcover in the United States by Scholastic Press in 2007.

ISBN-13: 978-0-439-87415-1   ISBN-10: 0-439-87415-7

12 11 10 9 8 7 6 5 4 3   8 9 10 11 12 13/0

Printed in the U.S.A.   23

First trade paperback printing, February 2008

PROLOGUE

Cavaliere Goldoni was famished.

He was as hungry as a wolf — not that there were any wolves in this country known as the Holy Land. Nor were there any other animals the Italian knight could have hunted and eaten. When Cavaliere Goldoni thought of the deer and wild boar that roamed the forest near his castle back home in Italy, his empty stomach rumbled as if a whole cavalcade of ghostly huntsmen were galloping through it.

Cavaliere Goldoni cursed the day he had let himself be talked into joining this Crusade against the Infidels. That was a year ago. Brother Francis had promised him that all his sins would be forgiven if he went. Well, he had no objection to that. But he hadn't gone to far-off Syria for that reason, nor for the sake of the riches that were said to be there for the taking. No, Cavaliere Goldoni had set off for the Holy Land because he had been promised everlasting honor and renown — and, above all, because he had been assured that a life of bloodshed and adventure was awaiting him there.

But what sort of life was he leading now?

More precisely, what had he been doing for the last two months?

Nothing.

He had been stuck in this hot, arid country for two whole months, doing nothing.

He wasn't entirely idle, of course. He rode out into the surrounding countryside again and again, searching for something to eat, or quarreled from sheer boredom with the other knights who, like him, lay encamped outside the walls of Sidon.

To be exact, they were besieging the place.

Together with their foot soldiers, Cavaliere Goldoni and another thirty-six Crusader knights from various European countries had surrounded the city and were waiting for its inhabitants to surrender.

The only trouble was, they had no intention of surrendering.

And Cavaliere Goldoni had to admit that they would have been very stupid to do so.

For one thing, the walls of Sidon were higher and stronger than he could ever have imagined back home. There was no hope of storming or destroying them, especially as the Crusaders possessed no catapults or other siege engines.

For another thing, Sidon was situated beside the sea.

The city had a well-protected harbor enclosed by high walls, and ships regularly arrived there, laden with all the supplies the inhabitants of Sidon needed in order to survive. The Crusader knights ground their teeth at this, but they could do nothing to prevent it, for they had no ships. Knights fought on land, not on water. They also fought on horseback — unless starvation compelled them to slaughter their horses for food.

So they lay encamped outside the walls of Sidon, condemned to hunger and inactivity, and waited for the city to surrender.

Which it wouldn't unless a miracle occurred.

And in Cavaliere Goldoni's opinion, the chances of a miracle were pretty slim.

Unlike him, Brother Francis believed in miracles.

Brother Francis, the little Mendicant friar, still potbellied despite the shortage of food . . . Brother Francis, the silver-tongued *preacher who could talk the hind leg off a donkey . . . Brother Francis, who had persuaded Cavaliere Goldoni to accompany him to this part of the world . . .*

Goldoni would dearly have liked to pay the monk back by thrashing him with the flat of his sword, but that, alas, was out of the question. Why? Because the Pope would someday make Francis a saint. Why? Because he understood the language of animals — or so he claimed. Although Goldoni didn't believe a word of this story, there might be something in it after all. So, it would be wiser not to hurt Francis. Or only a little.

In any event, Brother Francis, the tubby little monk, believed that a miracle would occur. He even believed that he could prove it.

He proclaimed that Goldoni and his band of knights were fighting on behalf of Almighty God, so what was to prevent the Almighty from giving them a helping hand? Francis firmly believed — so firmly, it was a foregone conclusion — that the Almighty would sooner or later see to it that some ships of his own appeared off Sidon. They had probably set sail a long time ago, laden with everything the Crusaders would need to storm and capture the city. Until the Almighty's ships turned up, they would simply have to grin and bear it.

In spite of their hunger and boredom.

Boredom on its own, Cavaliere Goldoni could have endured, but boredom combined with hunger was driving him crazy.

His stomach was rumbling. Deer and wild boar were just an impossible dream in this land.

But there had to be some animals you could eat, even here. Little beasts of the field — exotic rodents of some kind, perhaps.

By now, Cavaliere Goldoni would have eaten anything on four legs.

Anything — even the funniest, cutest little creature.

CHAPTER ONE

THEY WERE GENUINELY FUNNY.

Tears of mirth were streaming down the audience's cheeks. The humans playing the roles of Enrico and Caruso, the two guinea pigs, were first-class actors.

A gigantic staircase had been erected onstage, and the fat human impersonating Caruso was clinging to the edge of the top step.

"I don't dare let go!" he wailed. "I'll hurt myself!"

Enrico, played by a short, scrawny human, was standing below him on the next step down. He was bracing himself against Caruso's plump backside. "Come on, let go!" he cried. "I'll break your fall."

"Promise?"

"Cross my heart."

Caruso let go. He landed on top of Enrico with a thud, burying his skinny friend beneath him.

"HEY, GET OFF ME!" Enrico gasped. "I can't breathe!"

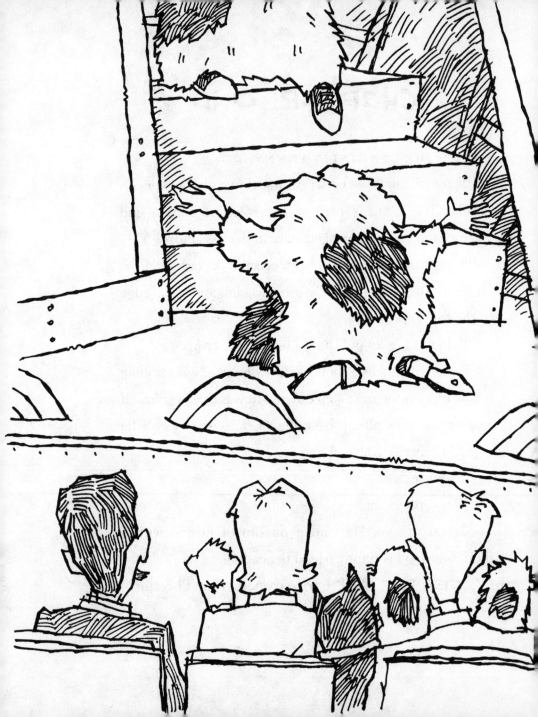

The audience rocked with laughter.

It was the first performance of *Freddy in Peril*, a stage play based on my book of the same name, and Mr. John and we animals had been invited to attend. So, of course, had Linda Carson, Mr. John's girlfriend. Our seats were in the front row, and I had chosen to watch the show perched on Linda's shoulder. The view would have been just as good from Mr. John's shoulder, but here I got a bonus: a delicious whiff of Linda's apple-and-peach-blossom scent. Perched on Mr. John's shoulders were Enrico and Caruso — the real ones — and seated at his feet was Sir William, the big, black, distinguished tomcat, who didn't need an elevated view of the stage.

Speaking of big and black, the seat next to Linda was

occupied by a man with a big, black mustache. Tall and slim, he was wearing a dark blue three-piece suit with a white handkerchief — silk, from the look of it — peeking out of his breast pocket just below the lapel. He looked very respectable.

And very expectant, too, although the play didn't seem to interest him in the least. He was apparently enthralled by something else. I sensed that he was eagerly awaiting the result of some experiment. Why had he come to the play at all? Why had he bought an expensive front-row seat? All the other grown-up members of the audience were parents accompanied by their children. All of them except this lone individual. **STRANGE.**

Meanwhile, up on the stage, Enrico and Caruso had lost their footing and slipped. They landed with an almighty crash. The audience roared with laughter.

They were really first-rate actors, both of them.

"They're hopeless," commented Enrico — the real Enrico, who sat perched on Mr. John's right shoulder.

Caruso nodded — the real Caruso, who was sitting on Mr. John's left shoulder. "Complete amateurs," he agreed.

"Talk about overacting!" said Enrico.

"You can say that again!" said Caruso. "*We* would never have made such fools of ourselves."

OH NO? They *had* made fools of themselves — that time when they and I and Sir William were escaping from Mr. John's apartment because Professor Fleischkopf, the horrible scientist, wanted to dissect my brain.

"Hey, you guys," I hissed at them, "pipe down, you're disturbing people."

"No, we aren't," said Enrico. "No one can hear us."

He was right. The two of them had been speaking Interanimal, the telepathic language all mammals can understand — all mammals except for humans, that is. To the rest of the audience, the guinea pigs perched on Mr. John's shoulders and the golden hamster on Linda's shoulder seemed to be sitting there in total silence.

"But *I* can hear you," I retorted angrily.

"YOU'RE DISTURBING ME."

"And you, my dear Freddy, are disturbing *me*." Sir William's big green eyes were gazing up at me. "So would you kindly be quiet?"

I nodded. "Of course." It was advisable to do as Sir William said, even when he asked you politely. A request from him was a command. Among us animals Sir William was the boss. For one thing, because of his size and impressively sharp teeth; for another, because of his wisdom and experience. (Not that this necessarily implies enormous mental ability. Only one of us four possesses *that*!) Unfortunately, His Lordship can be terribly unfair. He lets those guinea pigs get away with murder, whereas he had calmly told me off for doing just what they'd done.

"As for you two," Sir William went on, turning to Enrico and Caruso, "please be quiet too. Besides," he added, "a little less self-delusion would do you both good. Those two first-class actors are behaving precisely the way you did during our escape."

Enrico and Caruso hung their heads like a pair of guinea pigs busy ridding themselves of self-delusion.

Personally, I saw no reason to copy them, so I redirected my attention to what was happening onstage.

Enrico and Caruso had reached the bottom of the stairs. Professor Fleischkopf and Brewster, his sidekick, would appear at any moment.

Back then, the real Professor Fleischkopf's appearance had been heralded by a diabolical stench of sulfur (from his antidandruff shampoo), and . . .

WHaT Was THaT?

I straightened up and sniffed. Superimposed on Linda's apple-and-peach-blossom scent was the smell of plastic. No, not just plastic, plastic of the worst possible kind. It reeked — an affront to my hypersensitive golden hamster's nose. What was it that smelled so awful?

And where was the smell coming from?

The silk handkerchief! It wasn't there anymore. The dapper gentleman with the mustache had evidently removed it, and the smell of plastic was coming from his breast pocket, no doubt about it. (A golden hamster's nose can locate the source of a smell as accurately as a human eye can see a red balloon silhouetted against a whitewashed wall.) What on earth did the man have in his pocket?

Whatever it was, the smell was **UNBEARABLE.** To put some distance between it and me, I clambered around Linda's collar and perched on her other shoulder. Smell or no smell, I tried to concentrate on what was happening onstage.

The actors playing Enrico and Caruso dove into a hiding place beneath the stairs and reappeared a moment later in the roles of Professor Fleischkopf and Brewster.

Professor Fleischkopf shone his flashlight on the stairs. "Odd," he said, "I could have sworn I heard something."

"Well, I didn't," Brewster said loudly, just the way the real one had.

THaT SMELL oF PLaSTiC!

It had suddenly grown stronger — it had become a regular stench! I peered past the collar of Linda's blouse at the gentleman with the mustache.

Something was peeking out of his breast pocket. . . . A creature with golden-brown ears, eyes like black boot buttons, and whiskers sprouting from its nose . . .

I sat up on my haunches, ears pricked.

The creature was a golden hamster.

The next moment, it spotted me and ducked back into the pocket at lightning speed.

I slowly resumed my seat. The mustachioed gentleman had come to the theater accompanied by a golden hamster. . . .

IT JUST WASN'T POSSIBLE!

That's to say, of course it was. I was here myself, after all, but *I* was unique. In the first place, I was Freddy, the only golden hamster in the world who could read and write, and the author of no less than four books.

Secondly, I should have *smelled* the creature.

A golden hamster will always detect another member of its species at close range. The stench of plastic would never have drowned out that scent. My nose should have alerted me to the creature's presence.

How could that hamster stand to share the man's pocket with some plastic gizmo? *I* would have fainted from the fumes long ago.

So I was dealing with a hamster

18

that shouldn't by rights have existed: a golden hamster that not only didn't smell of golden hamster but was insensitive to other smells, notably the stench of plastic.

"Hey, hamster!" I called softly in Interanimal. "Show yourself again."

It didn't budge.

"You can come out. No one's going to hurt you."

Still no response.

Just then, applause rang out and the curtain came down. The intermission had begun.

The dapper gentleman with the black mustache got up and hurried out.

I had a lot to contend with during the intermission. Scores of children and their parents crowded around me (that's to say, around Linda, whose shoulder I was perched on) calling, "GIVE US A WAVE, FREDDY!", trying to stroke me, and begging for autographs. I was spared giving any autographs, luckily, because we'd left the laptop at home (a computer keyboard is the only hamster-friendly writing facility, as all my readers know). I spent the whole time looking around for the dapper gentleman with the black mustache, but I failed to spot him anywhere.

I couldn't wait to see if I would manage to coax the strange golden hamster out of his pocket again when the intermission was over.

But the seat beside Linda remained empty.

The dapper gentleman had left the theater.

The mystery of the scent-free, scent-proof golden hamster would never be solved.

OR SO I THOUGHT.

CHAPTER TWO

IT WAS AROUND HALF PAST NINE in the morning. I wanted to watch Mr. John at work, so I was sitting beside the keyboard of his Mac (the kind of computer a hamster's paw can turn on with ease). If any of my readers think I had no business to be sitting beside a computer at half past nine in the morning, they're absolutely right. We hamsters are "nocturnally active" creatures, as biology teachers say, so I should really have been tucked up asleep in my nest.

In fact, I was feeling as dozy as a human who has set his alarm clock for three a.m. (perhaps because he hasn't managed to finish his math homework the night before). Now that I think of it, living in Mr. John's apartment was like turning night into day from my point of view. Turning night into day is supposed to be very bad for you, so why did I do it all the same?

Because the rest of the family — Mr. John, Sir William, and Enrico and Caruso — were active during the day, and it would have bugged me to be asleep in my nest while everyone else was making a racket. Okay, so Mr. John and Sir William didn't "make a racket" — only Enrico and Caruso did that, and them I could happily have dispensed with — but I guess I've made my general meaning clear. At present, for instance, Mr. John was busy translating *Freddy in Peril* into German, and I was absolutely determined to watch him at work.

He was just tackling one of Enrico and Caruso's little ditties:

For computers we've no time at all,
nor for keyboards nor modems nor RAM.
We prefer to create what we call
our own entertainment program.

"Hmm," he muttered thoughtfully, plucking at one of his eyebrows. Mr. John has rather bushy eyebrows and a big nose to go with them. "It's going to be hard to make that rhyme in German. . . ."

Just then the telephone rang.

"Hello? — Sure, why not? — Want me to keep it a surprise? — No? Okay, see you soon." He hung up. "Freddy, guess who's coming to see you?"

At this time of day? It couldn't be Sophie, she was in school and her vacation didn't start till tomorrow. I darted over the keyboard, opened a new document, and typed, *No idea, Mr. John.*

"It's Sophie. Her class has been sent home early."

GREAT! SOPHIE WOULD BE PAYING ME A VISIT AFTER ALL!

SOPHIE, who smelled so appetizingly of sunflower seeds. SOPHIE, at whose home I had learned to read. SOPHIE, who had been my first mistress and remained so until I was relocated to Mr. John's apartment because her mom had developed an allergy to hamster fur. She has paid me regular visits ever since.

And she always brings a brown paper bag containing

a gift for me. I've a confession to make: Whenever Sophie produces that paper bag from her backpack, I can't help squeaking like a greedy little baby hamster.

But this time I *would* control myself, because this time *I* had a gift for *her*. And I would give it to her before she could take the bag from her b —

"Hello?" It was the phone again. "I see. — What about? — You can't tell me over the phone? — In that case, Mr. — Well then, Signor. — Sometime around noon, but I'm behind on a translation, so I can't spare you long, okay? — Good-bye, *arrivederci*." Mr. John hung up.

"Some Italian guy wants to see us. A Signor Goldoni. Any idea what it could be about?"

None, I typed.

And that was the plain truth. Up to then, at least.

A few minutes later I was comfortably curled up in

my nest, trying to grab some sleep after all. I wanted to be in good shape when Sophie came visiting.

In the beginning, when Sophie's father bought me at the pet shop and drove me to my new home, I was in far from good shape. I felt terribly nauseous in the car and almost threw up in my box. Since then I've gotten used to traveling by car, though it still makes me feel a trifle queasy. Automobiles aren't exactly the means of transportation nature intended for golden hamsters.

Go to sleep, I told myself.

Doing what nature intended was all very well, but I

was a civilized hamster, and that meant using human technological gadgets. Personally, I couldn't imagine life without a computer. Reading and writing had become my paradise on earth, my Promised Land of Assyria. . . .

25

Assyria! How long was it since that word had cropped up in my mind?

Assyria . . .

Great-Grandmother had told us about it in the pet shop's hamster cage. She had described the place in a hoarse, mysterious whisper while we youngsters hunkered down in the litter at the bottom of the cage, listening with hearts aflutter and stubby little tails erect.

aSSYRia, THE GOLDEN HamSTER'S PROMiSED LaND!

According to Great-Grandmother, Assyria had an abundance of soil that was neither too firm nor too loose, so you could dig tunnels in it to your heart's content without ever coming up against any bars or wire mesh. And the soil was full of earthworms ten times more delicious than the most succulent mealworm. On the soil's surface, fragrant fruit and all manner of grains and vegetables flourished at every season of the year, and they grew in such quantities that you could safely refrain from hoarding them. If you did wish to do so, however, you could dig yourself a storage chamber as big as the pet shop itself. The quality of the soil in the land of Assyria was so good that this presented absolutely no problem.

Great-Grandmother's voice suddenly changed: She was no longer whispering, in fact her tone was almost exultant. One wonderful day, she declared, all the golden hamsters in the world would be released from captivity and return to the Promised Land of Assyria. Then Golden Hamster Liberation Day, which was every golden hamster's dream, would dawn at last.

"**YOUNGSTERS**," cried Great-Grandmother, "**REJOICE!**"

And rejoice my fellow hamsters did. They bounded into the air, squeaking and cavorting around. As for me, I couldn't simply switch off my brain, even at that young age. How could all the golden hamsters in the world flock to Assyria on the same day, I wondered, and who would organize this mass migration? When I asked Great-Grandmother, she said she didn't know — in fact it turned out that she didn't even know whether the Promised Land of Assyria existed at all.

That was when I resolved to find my own way to freedom — to look for an Assyria of my own.

I found it by learning to read and write and living as a civilized, free-ranging golden hamster. It was a wonderfully satisfying existence. I couldn't conceive of a finer one.

Now go to sleep, I told myself.

BUT WHAT IF ASSYRIA EXISTS AFTER ALL?

Not, of course, Great-Grandmother's Promised Land — that was just a pie in the sky — but a country where a golden hamster might feel truly at home? A country adapted to a golden hamster's nature, so to speak? A country where he felt entirely at ease with himself?

Hey, enough soul-searching, time to grab some —

DING-DONG.

The doorbell! I heard Mr. John go to answer it and was out of my nest in a flash. I left my cage — the door is always open — then darted over to the desk and climbed my miniature rope ladder.

I reached the top just as Sophie burst into the study accompanied by her divine scent of sunflower seeds. "**FREDDY!**" she cried.

I sat up on my haunches and raised my right paw as high as I could. And then I waved to her (to the best of my knowledge, I'm still the only golden hamster in the world capable of greeting someone that way).

Sophie beamed at me. She's always so delighted to see me waving, you'd think she was seeing it for the very first time. Before she could reach into her backpack, however, I darted over to the keyboard.

Mr. John had kindly exited his translation and

left me a blank screen to write on.
I typed:

Sophie, dear, although I'm sorry
that we have to live apart,
waving to you is a token
that you're always in my heart.

Waving to you seals a friendship
made, I feel, in heaven above.
With this little salutation
I pledge my undying love.

Sophie didn't speak, just gazed at me earnestly. All at once, she did something she'd never done on any of her previous visits: She raised her right hand — not very high, roughly to shoulder level — and then, with a gentle, economical movement, she waved back.

30

I sat there without moving, thrilled to the core.

After a while she smiled, lowered her hand, and felt in her backpack.

THE PAPER BAG!

She removed the brown paper bag, opened it, and emptied its contents onto the desk in front of me.

It was a mealworm. A big, fat, segmented mealworm with bristly little feet. Above all, though, it was a *live* mealworm, and it was squirming around in front of me.

Maybe a civilized, domesticated, book-writing hamster shouldn't write about such things. Maybe he ought to tell himself: Okay, most people would be disgusted by what happens next, so I'll keep quiet about it.

But I think anyone who's reading a book written by a golden hamster should be made of sterner stuff, so here goes: I picked up the live mealworm with both front paws, saw and felt its segmented body and bristly little feet, saw and felt it squirming around. And then I popped it into my mouth and sank my teeth in it.

31

There's no more delicious sensation in the world than sinking your teeth into a live, squirming mealworm.

Sorry, but that's what comes naturally to a golden hamster.

Sophie had gone home and I was back beside the keyboard, watching Mr. John at work on his translation. But my thoughts were elsewhere. I kept seeing Sophie in my mind's eye — Sophie waving. Why had that thrilled me so much?

Perhaps because she'd done something only I did as a rule. She'd taken over my role, so to speak. It was almost as if she'd turned into a girl hamster. . . . But that was utter nonsense!

That's enough, I told myself.

CONCENTRATE!

I had wiped my poem from the screen (though not, of course, without saving it first), and Mr. John was debating how to translate something when I heard:

"On the battlements I tarry,
yearning for my knight's approach."

Enrico and Caruso were back in the Middle Ages again, it seemed. Those two comedians, who had been in a kind of medieval frenzy ever since our visit to the theater, were rehearsing one medieval romance after another. I sometimes wished I was as incapable of understanding Interanimal as Mr. John.

Enrico was hunkered down on the roof of the guinea pigs' cage. From the look of it, he was playing the role of a princess keeping watch for her sweetheart from the top of the castle tower. And, sure enough, here came Sir Caruso:

"Swiftly to thy side, sweet damsel,
filled with eagerness I race."

Whereupon Mistress Enrica called down from the battlements:

"Ah, with passion all aquiver
I await thy fond embrace."

Sir Caruso raised both paws in a theatrical gesture:

"I am likewise drunk with passion.
Let me in, my blood's on fire!"

Mistress Enrica:

"Would that I could, but no, I dare not
risk my noble father's ire."

Sir Caruso:

"Naught shall stop me. Let your hair down
and I'll use it as a rope."

Mistress Enrica:

"Father made me cut my tresses!"

Sir Caruso:

"Then we must abandon hope!"

Mistress Enrica, wringing her paws in despair:

"You mean our dreams will ne'er come true?"

Sir Caruso, turning away:

"So it seems. Well then, adieu. . . . Ciao, Sophie!"

Ciao, Sophie?

They'd done it again! Those jokers had poked fun at me yet again, and this time they hadn't left it at that. This time they'd had the gall to drag my love for Sophie in the mire of their guinea-piggish imagination. . . .

I SaW RED.

At top speed, I clambered down the rope ladder to the floor and sprinted over to the guinea pigs' cage.

Meantime, Enrico had left his castle tower. He and Caruso were sitting outside their cage, eyeing me with curiosity.

They hadn't a clue what they were in for.

I hadn't done it for a long time, but now I couldn't stop myself: I was going to flatten the pair of them.

I would rise up on my haunches, assume the hamster-in-attack stance, emit a bloodcurdling snarl, and — bingo! — those gagsters would fall flat on their backs, as helpless as a pair of upended dung beetles.

Why? Because guinea pigs are incapable of defending

against hamsterish aggression. Nature hasn't allowed for any confrontations between guinea pigs and hamsters, so Enrico and Caruso would give a terrible start and topple over backward.

It happened every time. Why? Because they always forgot that I'd flattened them before.

I reared up, blew out my cheeks in combat mode, and . . . **Ciao, THE PaiR OF YOU** . . .

Ciao, Sophie. . . .

I came down off my haunches.

That medieval romance of Enrico and Caruso's — idiotic though it was, hadn't they planted their inquisitive paws on my most vulnerable spot?

No matter how affectionately Sophie waved to me, she could never become a female hamster.

Sophie and I could never be an item.

I shook my head.

The guinea pigs' beady little eyes were watching me intently. All at once, Enrico said, "What's the matter, aren't you going to flatten us?"

37

I stared at him.

"Well," said Caruso, "carry on. We're waiting."

"Just a minute," I said, the truth slowly dawning on me. "You mean you've always known when I was going to —"

Ding-Dong!

It was probably Signor Goldoni. Mr. John went to open the door.

"All right," I went on, "come clean. Have you always . . ."

a SMELL.

I had detected a scent. A rather unpleasant one.

"Okay, you guys," I said hurriedly, "but you haven't heard the last of this."

Right now, I had something else on my mind.

WHY? BECAUSE MY NOSE HAD PICKED UP THE SMELL OF CHEAP PLASTIC.

CHapTer THREE

THE AIR STILL REEKED OF CHEAP PLASTIC ten
minutes later.

The difference was, we animals were now assembled
on Mr. John's desk. "Kids," he'd called, "there's something
we must discuss!" That was the signal for a family council
of war, and we always hold those beside the computer
because Mr. John can't tell what we're saying in
Interanimal unless I type it on the screen. Sir William
had jumped onto the desk, I had climbed up my rope
ladder, and Enrico and Caruso, who are about as good at
climbing as tortoises or potbellied Vietnamese pigs, had
been hoisted onto the desk by Mr. John. (But not before
he'd covered it with an old blanket, guinea pigs being
notoriously careless about where they relieve
themselves.) Mr. John was seated in his usual place.

The visitor's chair was occupied by Signor Goldoni.

His huge black mustache glistened as if it had been freshly waxed. He had exchanged his dark blue suit for an equally smart dark gray one, but today there was no handkerchief in his breast pocket. That, presumably, was why the disgusting smell of plastic — which was slightly less pungent than it had been in the theater — could fill the air unobstructed. But what on earth did the man keep in his pocket, and was the scent-free, scent-proof hamster in there too?

Ever since Goldoni's arrival, my mental command center had been issuing a Red Alert. A stranger was visiting us —a stranger who smelled repulsive! That was just how the Professor Fleischkopf business had started. Fleischkopf had come to survey our apartment.

WHY WAS GOLDONI* HERE?

I had failed to warn Mr. John against Professor Fleischkopf in good time. Well, I wouldn't make the same mistake twice. I sat at the keyboard with my paws poised.

Immediately after shaking hands with Mr. John, Goldoni had said, "It would be helpful, Signor, if Freddy, Sir William, and Enrico and Caruso took part in our conversation from the outset. That," he added with a smile, "would provide us with a combination of intelligence, wisdom, and wit."

His voice was pleasantly soft and deep, and he'd clearly done his homework on us. What was more, he'd mentioned me and intelligence first. However, he was wrong if he thought that would put me off my guard.

Goldoni opened the discussion by turning to me. "Freddy, *caro mio*," — "Freddy, my dear" won't work with me, I thought — "I can well imagine that this visit of mine reminds you of your first encounter with Professor Fleischkopf."

I STARED AT HIM IN SUPRISE.

He had obviously briefed himself thoroughly — and read *Freddy in Peril* with care.

"You have two questions for me, I imagine."

Well, well, I thought, so I do, do I? I can hardly wait to hear them, Signor Goldoni.

"For one thing, what is it in my pocket that smells so disgustingly of plastic? For another, what about the peculiar hamster that may also be lurking in there?"

I stared at him some more.

Then I shook my head. Don't let him hoodwink you, I told myself. But the man was no fool, and he certainly knew his stuff where golden hamsters were concerned. Still, the same had applied to Professor Fleischkopf.

"I promise to answer both those questions, *caro* Freddy, but may I keep you in suspense for a little while?" He looked at me as if he expected a reply. Okay, he could have one. *If you keep me waiting too long,* I typed, *I'll let you know. You can count on that.*

Goldoni smiled and nodded.

"I've come here," he said, surveying us all, "to invite the family to go on a journey."

"A journey?" Mr. John frowned. "What kind of journey? And what does 'the family' mean? Me and the animals?"

"*Scusi,* I expressed myself badly." Goldoni raised his hands in a gesture of apology. "I meant the animals only."

"Hmm." Mr. John shook his head. "Look, Signor Goldoni, I doubt the animals would want to — "

"It's a journey through time."

SiLENCE.

"A journey through time," Goldoni repeated. "A trip to another age."

Mr. John was still at a loss for words. So were we.

After a while — quite a while — Mr. John said, "If I understand you correctly, Signor Goldoni, you're talking about time travel. You're inviting the animals to travel to a time other than our own."

Goldoni nodded. "But only in the past. You can't visit the future unless you come from there."

"Of course not," Mr. John said sarcastically, "not unless you come from there." He rose to his feet. "I assume you aren't insane, Signor Goldoni, so I can only imagine this is a practical joke of some kind. I won't ask why you're playing it, I'll simply request you not to waste any more of my valuable time." He pointed at the door. "So, if you wouldn't mind . . ."

Goldoni had risen too. He sighed. "A pity. Now it will take me longer to convince you. I had hoped to whet your curiosity by launching a surprise attack, so to speak." He looked Mr. John in the eye. "You're right, I'm not insane, but I'm not joking either. Would it be expecting too much, Signor, if I asked you — just for interest's sake — to consider a third alternative?"

"THE POSSIBLITY OF TIME TRAVEL, YOU MEAN?"

Goldoni nodded. "I've discovered how it can be done."

Mr. John was still on his feet but no longer pointing at the door. "Have you any proof? Convincing proof, I mean?"

Goldoni shook his head. "I'm afraid you must simply take my word for it."

"Why should I?"

"Perhaps because you would be saving someone's life."

Mr. John slowly resumed his seat. Goldoni sat down too.

Mr. John eyed him keenly. "You don't look like a practical joker." He sighed. "Okay, my work will have to wait. So who's this person whose life is in danger?"

"My son. He's suffering from a rare blood disease — one from which he will die in the very near future. This disease is caused by a genetic defect that has often recurred in our family. It's incurable — or has been until now. However, if it were possible to obtain some genetic material, some DNA, from a direct ancestor of ours who was born before the disease first manifested itself, a cure for it could be developed. Luckily, we can trace our family tree a very long way back. Back to the twelfth century, in fact."

Just then, Enrico and Caruso exchanged a glance. Could the two of them have grasped something that hadn't yet occurred to me?

IT WAS CONCEIVABLE.

Not because guinea pigs are more intelligent than hamsters — far from it — but because I was preoccupied. I was still trying to work out what Goldoni was really up to. Why was he holding out on me? Why wouldn't he reveal the source of that awful smell?

"I'm a physicist," he was saying. "I'm also lucky enough to have inherited a large fortune. All my energies and financial resources have been devoted to solving the problem of time travel."

"And you believe you've cracked it?"

"I *know* I have," said Goldoni.

Silence.

"Okay," said Mr. John, "let's assume you're right. Why come to us? Why should these animals make the trip? Why not go and get this ancestral DNA yourself?"

"That's just the point." Goldoni fitted his fingertips together. "I've discovered that humans can't travel through time. Do you know why?"

"No, but I'm sure you're going to tell me," Mr. John said with a faint smile. He was obviously developing a liking for this oddball. I hadn't reached that stage myself, far from it.

"It's always the same old problem, as sci-fi readers are well aware," said Goldoni, warming to his subject. "Someone travels back into the past, does something there that changes the course of history, and returns to the present — which has also been changed as a result. Perhaps he goes back again and gives history another little nudge. The result? **CHaos.** *Una grande confusione*, know what I mean?"

Mr. John's smile broadened. He nodded.

"It's all nonsense, of course," Goldoni went on. "The present can't be altered retrospectively. If people *could* travel back into the past, their journey would have to be as ineffectual as if they'd never been there at all. **NOW PAY ATTENTION!**" He raised his index finger. "The opposite conclusion applies. If people can only visit the past without changing anything, it means they're *incapable* of traveling there. Logical, no?" Goldoni stroked his mustache. "I call that the **GOLDONIAN LAW OF TIME TRAVEL.**"

Mr. John smiled again. "So what about animals?"

"Animals can't change anything. They have no history and exert no cultural influence. . . ." Goldoni broke off and turned to me. "Oh, *scusi, scusi*! Any animal who writes books *does* exert a cultural influence, no doubt about it. But it's not exactly typical of a golden hamster to do so, is it?" I shook my head. Signor Goldoni had a point. But his pocket was still emitting a smell of plastic, and if he didn't disclose the source of the stench before long I would insist on being told the truth with all the force at my command.

"But animals, too, are subject to a certain limitation," Goldoni continued, turning back to Mr. John. "Can you guess what it is?"

"Hmm . . ." Mr. John thought this over. "Perhaps animals can travel back only to a time when their species already existed."

"Precisamente!" Goldoni clapped his hands. "To be more exact: Genetically speaking, their species must have mutated to only a limited extent. According to my calculations, animals alive today can travel back into the past for no more than eight hundred and fifty years."

Enrico and Caruso exchanged another glance, heaven alone knew why. They were obviously picking up something that eluded me. I resolved to pay greater attention.

"Well," said Mr. John, "that all sounds quite believable. I won't ask you about the technicalities of such a journey — I wouldn't understand them anyway."

He looked at Goldoni. "Have you actually constructed a time machine, or something similar?"

"Or something similar, yes." Goldoni grinned. "The outward journey requires a pretty large and complicated apparatus. For the return journey a smaller device will be good enough. A very much smaller one." He paused. "I've brought it with me."

"Really? May we see it?"

"Of course," Goldoni replied. Then he said,

"TJARK* BE GOOD ENOUGH TO SHOW YOURSELF."

At that, the strange golden hamster peeked out of his breast pocket.

*Tjark: pronounced CH-ARK

CHAPTER FOUR

THE GOLDEN HAMSTER WASN'T A GOLDEN HAMSTER at all.

The scent-proof golden hamster was a machine!

a TiME MaCHiNE.

Carefully, Goldoni removed it from his pocket and deposited it on the desk beside me. "Tjark, this is Freddy. Freddy, meet Tjark."

We stared at each other.

It *was* a golden hamster. Everything was right: the ears, the black boot-button eyes, the whiskers, the fur. It looked exactly like a golden hamster. And, exactly like a golden hamster, it proceeded to groom its fur.

Everything was right — except for one minor detail.

It didn't smell like a golden hamster.

It smelled of plastic. Overpoweringly so.

Tjark, the mechanical hamster, stank as if someone had turned on ten cheap TV sets at once.

"It's his fur," said Goldoni. "Unfortunately, the only way I could reproduce the texture of golden hamster fur was to use a strong-smelling man-made fiber."

"I predict that the odor will fade," Tjark said suddenly. "I estimate that the emission of odorous substances will soon have diminished by approximately ninety percent."

Oh, great, only one smelly TV set . . . Just a minute! I shook my head to clear it.

Tjark had spoken. Really spoken, I mean. Spoken aloud —SPOKEN LIKE a HUMAN!

He hadn't used Interanimal.

"He can't," said Goldoni, who had evidently read my mind. "How could he? I don't know Interanimal myself — no human does — so I couldn't teach it to him."

"But I'm quite capable of learning it," said Tjark, adopting the sit-up-and-beg position. "I was designed to be a superintelligent machine."

SUPERINTELLIGENT, HUH?

I would soon show him who was superintelligent around here. I rose on my haunches too.

"I've equipped him with an autodidactic brain," Goldoni said hurriedly. "He'll soon master Interanimal — and, if need be, any human language as well."

"Even languages that are no longer spoken today," Tjark put in. "I already know one."

Enrico and Caruso exchanged yet another glance and stiffened expectantly.

"The language to which I refer," Tjark went on, "is the Old French spoken by the Crusaders."

"HURRaH, SO iT'S TRUE!"

cried Caruso. "We're going back to the age of chivalry!"

"We'll rub shoulders with noble, valiant knights!" Enrico said exultantly. "Real, live ones."

"And make the acquaintance of delightful highborn damsels," gushed Caruso. "And they won't be playacting!"

"It'll be a dream come true!" Enrico enthused.

The guinea pigs joined paws and proceeded to perform a kind of courtly minuet.

"Freddy," said Mr. John, "what's the matter with Enrico and Caruso? They seem to have developed itchy feet."

They can't wait to pay a visit to the age of chivalry, I typed on the keyboard.

"Oh!" Goldoni exclaimed. "Did I forget to mention it?" He turned to the guinea pigs. "*You* won't be going, I'm afraid."

"**WHAT?!**" shrieked Enrico.

"**WHY NOT?**" yelled Caruso.

I translated for them: *The guinea pigs would like to know why not.*

"You *could* go, in theory," Goldoni replied, "but you'd be a geographical impossibility. Guinea pigs did exist eight hundred and fifty years ago, but only in South and Central America."

"So what?" cried Enrico.

"What's wrong with that?!" Caruso demanded loudly.

I wrote Caruso's question on the monitor, leaving out the exclamation mark.

"I don't know, to be honest." Goldoni shook his head. "It might work out all right. On the other hand, you might disappear into the space-time continuum — a kind of black hole — and never be seen again." He made a regretful gesture. "*Scusate,* but it's too risky. The two of you must stay behind."

Enrico and Caruso flattened like a pair of deflated balloons. It was positively pitiful — or so I would have thought if I hadn't felt rather relieved. I had no objection to time travel, but I was dead against traveling through time in their company. Time travel with guinea pigs is bad for hamsters (Freddy's First Law of Time Travel).

Goldoni turned to me and Sir William. "I had only the two of you in mind from the outset," he said. "It would be wonderful if you agreed to go."

Without Enrico and Caruso?

YOU BET! ANYTIME!

Sir William said nothing even now. He nodded, but only faintly. Did he have some secret misgivings? Did he, for instance, think that . . . One moment!

Why did I take it for granted that this trip into the past would be free from danger for him and me?

Signor Goldoni, I typed, *can you guarantee that no harm will come to me and Sir William?*

Goldoni shook his head. "I can guarantee nothing. You'll be the first to undertake such a journey. However," he went on, "having carefully weighed all the risks, I think I can — as a scientist — assume the responsibility for sending you on it."

He *thought* he could. . . . As a *scientist* . . .

All at once, from my memory bank of smells, there arose a recollection of Professor Fleischkopf's sulfurous stench. He, too, had been a scientist — a cruel, unscrupulous, treacherous one. What made me think that Goldoni was being straight with us?

HaD I LET HiM BaMBOOZLE ME?

Even if his son really had this disease (Mr. John would naturally check that out), it was still possible that Sir William and I were to be sacrificed on this pioneering journey through time. As experimental guinea pigs, so to speak.

Saving someone's life was one thing, losing my own in the process was another.

Just as this was going through my mind, Goldoni asked, "Well, Freddy, where do you think I'm proposing to send you?"

To see some ancestor of yours in Italy, I typed. Except I wasn't going anywhere.

"The ancestor I have in mind isn't . . ." Goldoni broke off and smiled. "I mean, of course, *wasn't* in Italy eight hundred and fifty years ago."

Oh? I typed — purely for courtesy's sake, because I considered the matter closed.

"At the present time — that's to say, eight hundred and fifty years ago — he's a Crusader in the Holy Land."

The Holy Land?

"In Syria." Goldoni paused. "You might also say: in *Assyria*."

59

Bamboozled or not, I'd taken his bait — hook, line, and sinker. I was determined to go to Assyria.

But I had to save face, so I asked for time to think it over and retired to my nest. Ten minutes' thought struck me as long enough, but I added another five to be on the safe side. Then I climbed back onto the desk and wrote *Deal* on the screen.

"*Va bene!*" Signor Goldoni exclaimed.

"BRAVO, FREDDY!"

He was looking highly relieved. It was clear that he'd been genuinely afraid I would turn him down. Or was he only playacting? Had he been banking on his trump card, "Assyria," from the very first?

No matter. The fact was, Sir William and I would soon be —

"Freddy, old boy," said Sir William, breaking in on my thoughts, "would you mind giving Signor Goldoni a message from me?"

"With pleasure."

"Kindly inform him as follows: I'll come on this trip, but only on one condition."

Enrico and Caruso, who were stretched out on the blanket looking disconsolate, pricked up their ears for some reason.

"I'll come," Sir William went on, "but only if Enrico and Caruso come too."

The guinea pigs beamed at each other.

"But Sir William," I said, "why on earth? I mean, what do we want with those two?"

"Look, my dear fellow, would you kindly tell Signor Goldoni exactly what I just said — without any more personal remarks?"

"Of course," I said, and proceeded to type out his message.

The time travel operation would be a nonstarter without Sir William, I reflected while typing. We might have to cover a lot of ground in Syria. Being as small as I am, I can do this only by gripping the back of Sir William's neck with my teeth and getting him to carry me. Goldoni knew this, of course, but how did he imagine Tjark would make out? Did he think I'd let him ride beside me on Sir William's back? (Which was out of the question anyway, if only for reasons of space.) That smelly, conceited mechanical hamster was liable to ruin my trip to Syria in any case, and if those two comedians came as well . . . Never mind, I felt sure that Goldoni would talk Sir William into withdrawing his condition. He was a smooth-talking Italian, after all. . . .

"It's a deal," said Goldoni — *too* smoothly.

The guinea pigs seized each other's paws and performed a ridiculous jig.

Goldoni smiled. Turning to Sir William, he went on, "May I ask what prompted you to make that condition?"

WHaT iNDEED?! His Lordship didn't like going anywhere without his two court jesters.

"Please write him the following reply," Sir William asked me. "All animals are entitled to decide what risks they take. To dictate to them as if they're babes in arms is incompatible with their dignity."

Dignity? Enrico and Caruso? **WHaT a LaUGH!**

However, I refrained from commenting and typed Sir William's animal-rights declaration on the keyboard.

Goldoni nodded gravely. "I hadn't thought of that. Please forgive me."

Sir William responded with a nod and a gracious "GRANTED!"

I had a question I wanted answered — a pretty important question, in my mind — but Mr. John said, "Wait a minute."

"Er, wait?" said Goldoni. "What do you mean?"

"What I mean is, this is all happening far too fast for my taste. I'm responsible for these animals, after all." He looked at Goldoni. "Your son's life is at stake, but so are theirs. I'd like to be certain that nothing will happen to them on the journey."

"I've weighed all the risks, as I already said, carefully and in full awareness of my responsibilities." Goldoni fell silent for a moment. "However, Signor, I'm unable to give you the assurance you seek."

"Freddy," said Sir William, "would you please tell

Mr. John that we animals are prepared to accept the risks involved in such a journey?"

I typed the words.

"And you're a hundred-percent sure?" Mr. John eyed us closely. "All four of you?"

We nodded. Vigorously. All four of us.

"In that case, so be it. I agree."

Signor Goldoni breathed a sigh of relief.

I was able to ask my question at last. *Signor Goldoni,* I typed, *what will Tjark do if we have to cover long distances?*

Goldoni turned to him. "Tjark, be good enough to demonstrate how you cover long distances."

The electronic hamster went down on all fours. I suddenly heard a faint **HiSSSSSSSS** — inaudible to human ears, no doubt — and Tjark took off. He hovered a paw's-breadth above the desk, **ZOOOOOOOOMED** over the keyboard to the edge, then turned and **ZOOOOOOOOMED** back again. Then he slowly lowered himself onto all fours and the hiss died away.

65

"This part of my locomotor system was designed like a hovercraft," he announced. "It's a considerable improvement on the hovercraft principle, of course."

Oh, sure. I was developing more and more of a dislike for this plastic traveling companion of mine.

"Hmm," said Mr. John. "He can think, speak, and move around — he even hovers on a cushion of air. . . . I guess that must use up a lot of energy."

Goldoni's face darkened. "You've put your finger on a sore point, Signor. Although I've managed to develop a new form of fuel cell, the energy it can store is limited."

"How long will it last?"

"Thirty-six hours at the most. Less, if Tjark has to levitate for any length of time. A lot less, depending on circumstances."

"Hmm," Mr. John said again. "I don't mean to criticize, but wouldn't it have been better to design the machine in the form of a bigger animal with room for more fuel cells?"

Goldoni shook his head. "For one thing, its energy consumption would have been greater. For another, I wanted to make Tjark as inconspicuous as possible. My ancestor is in an area where rodents are few and far between. Even Enrico and Caruso will attract attention because of their size — not to mention Sir William."

What kind of animals live there? I typed.

Goldoni stared at me in surprise. "But Freddy, can't you guess?"

Could I? Yes, of course I could!

I smote my brow with my paw.

WE WERE GOING TO ASSYRIA!

Not to the legendary Assyria of which Great-Grandmother had spoken in hushed tones, but to the real place.

We were going to Syria.

The home of the Syrian golden hamster.

CHAPTER FIVE

THE DAY OF OUR DEPARTURE had dawned at last.

Today Linda was going to drive us to Goldoni's laboratory.

Three weeks had gone by since his first visit to us. Why so long? Had Tjark taken all that time to learn Interanimal?

I wish I could say that, but he learned it much quicker. Very much quicker. If the truth be told, that computerized creature mastered our telepathic language within minutes, simply by listening to us. He really was a superintelligent machine, and I couldn't afford to let it upset me anymore. That would have been as stupid as a human getting annoyed with an extremely powerful computer that trounces him at chess every time.

But at least a chess computer keeps its trap shut and doesn't get on your nerves with its ultra-clever remarks. For instance, Tjark had the nerve to tell me: "I consider it appropriate to draw your attention to that fact that you

68

groom your fur too often. Animals of the genus *Mesocricetus auratus* groom their fur less frequently than you do." He even treated me to the following information: "*Mesocricetus auratus* is the scientific name for the golden hamster."

"That," I said, trying to sound duly sarcastic, "is not exactly news to me."

To which Tjark replied solemnly, "I mention the fact only because it doesn't form part of a normal golden hamster's store of knowledge."

"BUT I'M NOT a NORMaL GOLDEN HaMSTER!"

"I see no reason why you should raise your voice when making such a remark," Tjark retorted. "That was merely a statement for the record," he added, "not a comment on the fact that outbursts are a symptom of uncontrolled anger."

I gritted my teeth and said no more. Tjark was a know-it-all and a pain in the neck, but there's no point in quarreling with a computer.

Unlike me, Sir William got along

well with him. He didn't seem to worry about the electronic hamster's unusual characteristics and simply accepted him as he was. Mind you, Tjark never lectured Sir William on fur cleaning!

And Enrico and Caruso? If I needed any further proof that Tjark wasn't a genuine hamster, it was *this*: He became friends with the guinea pigs — firm friends. He was always sitting in their cage with them. I should add that their litter is always on the damp side, so it stinks like . . . Enough said! But that didn't worry Tjark. It was clear that Signor Goldoni had either failed or considered it unnecessary to equip his mechanical creature with a hamster's nose that was worthy of the name. A grave deficiency, in my opinion. Be that as it may, I wasn't the least bit interested in what the three of them were up to.

I paused to listen outside the guinea pigs' cage only once, while on my way to see Sir William, who sleeps on a blanket in Mr. John's bedroom. I'd heard Enrico say, like a schoolkid in class: "*Le chevalier* — the knight."

"No," said Tjark, "I advise you to modify your

pronunciation
of the final syllable.
The word is pronounced
'chevalyay,' not 'chevaleer.'"

GOOD HEAVENS, couldn't that superintelligent machine bring himself to speak normally for once?

Enrico repeated the word in accordance with Tjark's instructions.

"*Le tournoi* — the tournament," Caruso recited.

Tjark nodded. "Very good. Your pronunciation of the word is perfectly in keeping with the way people spoke in those days."

Why were the guinea pigs learning this stuff? After all, Tjark would promptly translate everything from Old French into Interanimal. I walked on, shaking my head.

71

I myself had also started learning — or rather, reading — about Syria in the twelfth century. I wanted to know all there was to know about the place. But then Goldoni mentioned that Tjark naturally possessed a data bank containing every available item of information on the subject. That was when I gave up, I must admit. Why bother to learn anything when I had a computer I could consult? All the same, I felt uncomfortable. What would I have thought of schoolkids who said they didn't need to learn anything because they could get it all from the Internet?

But to revert to the question of why so much time went by between Goldoni's first visit and the day of our departure. As I already said, this had nothing to do with Tjark's ability to learn Interanimal. The problem was his power supply.

"I'm worried by his limited storage capacity," Mr. John had told Goldoni during his first visit. "It could be

 DANGEROUS."

"You're right," Goldoni had said, nodding. "I'll try to improve his fuel cell." Then he departed — without Tjark, who was instructed to become thoroughly acquainted with us. According to Goldoni, this would be a complicated process in spite of the numerous chips he'd installed in Tjark's body. "Each of you is a miniature universe," he said. "Tjark is being continuously bombarded with vast quantities of new information. To be honest, I doubted his ability to absorb it sufficiently during our recent visit to the theater."

After three weeks, Goldoni had managed to increase Tjark's storage capacity from thirty-six to forty-eight hours maximum. Although Mr. John greeted this news with a dubious shake of the head, Sir

William and I were prepared to take the risk. So were Enrico and Caruso, whose crash course in Old French had made them twice as keen to visit the age of chivalry.

Oh yes, I forgot: Tjark's stench of plastic really had faded. I doubt if it was only one tenth as strong as before, but I could now bear to be near him — at least where my nose was concerned.

Linda, wearing her delightful apple-and-peach-blossom perfume as usual, turned up around noon and drove us to the town where Goldoni's laboratory was situated. Her car was an economical little compact, and Mr. John squeezed into the passenger seat with his knees drawn up. We animals sat crowded together on the shelf at the rear (Tjark had been collected by Goldoni two days earlier). I was feeling rather queasy again. So, incidentally, was Sir William.

Enrico and Caruso were sitting with their noses pressed up against the rear window, watching the countryside speed past. Unlike us, they were in the best of spirits. I eyed them suspiciously. Whenever Linda

was driving us someplace in her car and they were gazing out the window, as happy as could be, they came up with —

"**a SONG!**" cried Enrico. "Let's sing a song, Caruso, you divinely talented troubadour!"

"**YES, a SONG!**" cried Caruso. "You always sense my innermost desires, Enrico, you equally divinely talented troubadour!"

"Not a good idea, guys." I tried to strike a friendly note so as to get Sir William on my side. "We've got some tiring time travel ahead of us, so you'd best go easy on yourselves. On me, too, not to mention Sir William."

"Oh, thanks for being so concerned," said Enrico, "but I think an amusing little song would cheer us all up."

And away they went:

Life is a pleasure trip, my friends,
enjoy it while you may.
If you don't make the most of it,
you'll often rue the day.
"It's pointless to feel blue!" – so
say Enrico and Caruso.

We're going in a time machine
another age to see.
No matter what awaits us there,
or what the end may be.
"It's pointless to feel blue!" – so
say Enrico and Caruso.

For timid hamsters everywhere
we have a useful tip:

Don't be depressed or sad or scared,
press on and just let rip.
"It's pointless to feel blue!" – so
say Enrico and Caruso.

Me, a *timid* hamster?!

BY aLL THE . . . !

I sprang to my feet, fur standing on end. To think that those bed-wetting guinea pigs dared to . . . Okay, you guys, want me to let it rip? You asked for it! Let's see how you feel *then*! I reared up on my haunches and —

"Freddy, my friend," Sir William said softly, "cool it, would you?"

Okay, I told myself, cool it. **OKaY, OKaY!!!**

But sooner or later I *would* let it rip — those two could depend on *that*.

To get to Goldoni's laboratory, Linda had to drive into the industrial section of the town. She pulled up outside the entrance of an inconspicuous building no different

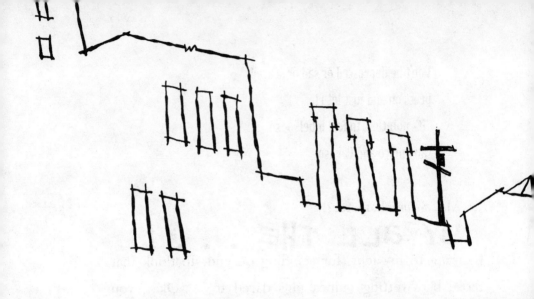

from the other factories around it. No one would have guessed that it contained an invention as brilliant as a time machine.

"For one thing, the machine takes up a certain amount of space," Mr. John explained. "For another, Goldoni wants to keep it under wraps. He isn't planning to exploit his invention in the interests of science, still less to make money out of it. It serves only one purpose." He turned around and looked at us. "He has

78

asked me to tell you this: Don't feel pressured by his son's illness, and don't risk your lives because of it. Simply do whatever you can do safely and then come back. Okay?"

We nodded, but I sensed that our mission would be a tough one.

Just then, Goldoni emerged from the building. He was wearing a white laboratory gown, and perched on his shoulder was — a golden hamster.

It was Tjark, of course, but the sight of that electronic

hamster took my breath away at first, it was so lifelike.

"Good morning, Freddy," said Tjark. "I note that your fur is bristling slightly. From this I infer that you recently allowed feelings of anger to get the better of you."

And I, you bag of silicone chips, note that you still haven't learned to speak normally. From this I infer that, in one respect at least, you're a pretty dumb box of tricks.

"Hi, Tjark, old buddy!" cried Enrico. "How goes it?"

"Our days have lacked that vital spark," rhymed Caruso, "without the presence of our old pal Tjark."

To which Tjark responded: "Hi, You pair of Litterpiddlers*!"

*Litterpiddlers: creatures who urinate on their cage beddings (yuck!)

So he *had* learned how to speak normally!

Enrico and Caruso squealed with delight. Tjark was a chum after their own hearts.

"Freddy," said Tjark, "I cannot help noting, yet again, that your fur is on the point of bristling with rage."

COOL IT, FREDDY.

He's just a kind of chess computer incapable of speaking normally unless he activates the chip that governs his conversations with Enrico and Caruso.

The three humans had naturally overheard none of this (the fact that they can't pick up Interanimal is regrettable from one angle, but it also spares them a lot of aggravation). Having welcomed us, Goldoni said, "When we go inside the factory you'll see a lot of perfectly ordinary-looking machines — generators, for instance. The time machine itself you'll recognize at a glance."

He opened the sliding door and we went inside, I on Linda's shoulder, Enrico and Caruso on Mr. John's, and Sir William on his own four paws. . . .

The time machine was spherical.

It was a shiny silver globe so huge that it almost touched the roof and rested on some sturdy supports. At the bottom — the south pole, so to speak — was a circular entrance.

"What you see here," said Goldoni, "is the outer shell of a hollow sphere. Inside it, at its exact center, is a second hollow sphere, the time capsule where all the energy is concentrated. The diameter of the inner sphere is roughly this big." He held up his hands about two feet apart. "It's your point of departure." He smiled. "And, of course, the point at which you'll reappear."

We went over to a table with a laptop on it. *Is the rest of the outer sphere empty?* I typed.

Goldoni shook his head. "Picture the interior as a labyrinth, but a spherical one. Your time capsule is shielded from all outside influences by a maze of gravitational fields."

"GRavitational SHMavitational,"

said Enrico. "Who cares?"

"You said it, pal," Caruso chimed in. "Freddy, ask the signor how soon it is to liftoff."

The guinea pigs are of the opinion, I wrote on the screen, *that you're being too theoretical. They want to get cracking.*

Goldoni grinned. "Spoken like true South American adventurers," he said. Then he looked grave. "There's a bit more theory to come," he told Enrico and Caruso, "but don't worry, it only involves a couple of points." He looked at them closely. "They're important to your survival."

Enrico and Caruso said nothing.

The guinea pigs are of the opinion, I typed, *that they want to survive.*

"Bene," said Goldoni. He then addressed us all. "The machine opens a time channel. This comes out at a particular moment in the past, but also at a particular place. You can return here only from that spot, and only in Tjark's company. Unless you get back there in good time, you'll be trapped in the past."

Goldoni proceeded to tug at his luxuriant mustache. "As you know, Tjark's store of energy will run out after forty-eight hours at the most, probably far sooner. He'll always know how much time you've got left." He thought for a moment. "Tjark won't be operational immediately on arriving in the past. His system must first collect and process all the data relating to your new environment. You animals won't be ready to go into action either, because you'll feel sick — very sick, in fact. How long this feeling of nausea will take to wear off I don't know — several minutes, I guess. During that time you'll be incapable of reacting to your new surroundings."

Another pause. "Several minutes aren't a long time here and now," he went on, "but in the past they could make the difference between life and death. Who knows? You may come to rest only inches from an extremely venomous scorpion."

Goldoni paused again, then turned to Enrico and Caruso. "I must remind you two that you'll be a geographical impossibility. You may even fail to arrive at all. Do you still want to go?"

"Definitely," Enrico said without hesitation.

"You bet," Caruso amplified. They both nodded so vigorously that I was spared having to translate.

"*Bene.*" Goldoni let go of his mustache. "Now to your mission. I need something from my ancestor's body — a scrap of fingernail, a hair, or something similar. But you must be a hundred percent certain that it comes from him. Unless you can guarantee that on your return, the mission will have been a failure."

Another pause.

"I don't know exactly where in Syria my ancestor is," Goldoni went on. "However, the time machine has stored so much information about him, it will be able to land you in his vicinity. You may find yourselves in the desert, in the barren mountains of the interior, or in the fertile coastal strip, so be prepared for anything." He looked at each of us in turn. "Any questions?"

I shook my head. Sir William had no questions either, nor had Enrico and Caruso.

"In that case . . ." Goldoni was just about to turn off the laptop when something occurred to me.

This ancestor of yours, I typed. *What's his name?*

"My ancestor's name?" Goldoni looked first at the screen and then at me. "You mean I've never told you that?" He shook his head. "My ancestor is a Crusader knight. He's known as the

CAVALIERE GOLDONI."

CHAPTER SIX

IT WAS A PEACEFUL ENVIRONMENT.

No, peaceful was a pale description of it.

There were sounds, of course. The hum of insects, the rustle of some creature nearby, but aside from that it was quiet.

No roar of traffic, no airplanes droning overhead . . .

I suddenly became aware that my ears, my hypersensitive golden hamster's ears, had been continuously bombarded with sounds in the world I'd left behind. I don't just mean the hum of the refrigerator in Mr. John's apartment or the ticking of his alarm clock. I mean the never-ending background noise that polluted the silence. Here it was lacking.

THE aiR WaS FRaGRaNT.

It was laden with many scents — the scents of plants and flowers — and they all went together like the notes of a musical composition, a blend of fragrances that seemed strangely familiar to me.

It was warm too.

A human would have found it hot, but to me the air felt warm and balmy. It struck me that the temperature was exactly as it ought to be at this time of year.

I felt as at home here as a golden hamster in . . . hmm.

I couldn't remember a thing about the trip. One minute we were sitting in the time capsule;

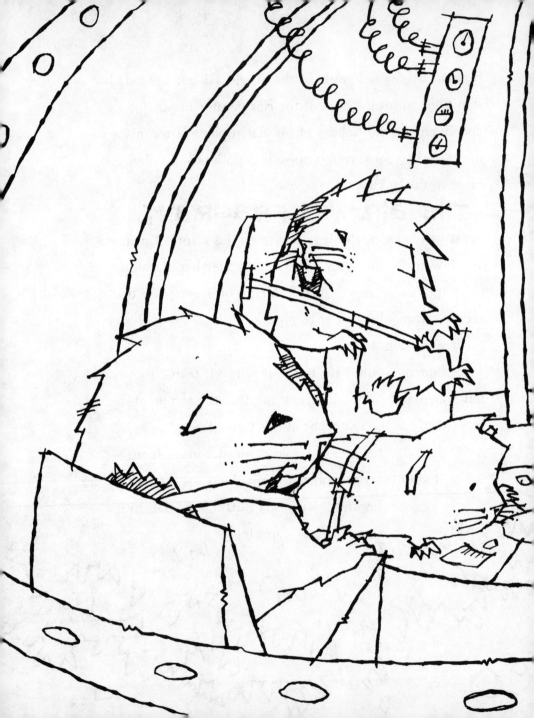

now we were here. We landed just as we'd taken off, with Sir William sitting beside me and Enrico and Caruso facing us.

They hadn't been swallowed up by the space-time continuum (a tribute to the space-time continuum's good taste) and were grinning at each other.

Lying between them was Tjark. He was stretched out on his stomach with his eyes shut, collecting and processing data.

But hadn't Goldoni said we would feel sick? I felt fine. So did Enrico and Caruso, from the look of them. Likewise Sir William.

Nor had we landed only inches from an extremely venomous scorpion. We were sitting beneath a bush whose overhanging branches provided us with excellent cover.

"Let's see what the world outside looks like," said Enrico.

"Wait till Tjark is back in action," I wanted to say — but then it flooded over me, a feeling of nausea such as I had never experienced before. I wasn't merely on the verge of throwing up; I seemed to feel every last fiber of my body, and every last fiber felt horribly nauseous. I lay curled up on the ground. If an extremely  venomous scorpion had chosen that moment to attack me, I would have been utterly indifferent to its attentions.

I was equally indifferent to the pitiful groans Sir William was making beside me. As for Tjark, he didn't stir.

"Well, what do you know!" I heard Enrico exclaim. "**MASSES OF TENTS!**"

"They're knights' pavilions," said Caruso. "It's a regular encampment."

I could vaguely see Enrico and Caruso peeking out through the foliage. Those two geographical impossibilities were clearly *not* feeling sick, but I didn't care about that either. I shut my eyes.

"And that city over there!" I heard Enrico say. "Gee, what huge walls!"

"Knights' pavilions, city walls . . . **BOY, OH BOY!**" Caruso cried delightedly. "Know what's going on here, fellow time traveler? It's a siege! They're Crusaders besieging a city in the Holy L**—EEEK!**"

A simultaneous "**EEEK!**" came from Enrico. I heard a sudden rustle of leaves followed by footsteps — a man's receding footsteps, from the sound of them. I opened my eyes with an effort.

"What was that?" asked Tjark, opening his eyes too. He sat up.

"No idea." My nausea had suddenly left me. I felt as I had just after we landed.

"I'm afraid, my friends, that Enrico and Caruso are in some kind of trouble." Sir William rose and peered through the branches. "Good heavens!"

I looked out too.

It really was a man. A tubby little man wearing a monastic habit. He'd hitched it up and was clasping it to his belly. There was something in his arms.

The fat little monk had snatched up Enrico and Caruso and was carrying them away!

"Oh dear," sighed Tjark. A perfectly normal reaction. He'd obviously activated his E & C chip.

"I fear this incident will complicate our mission considerably," Sir William remarked. He'd obviously activated his thought processes.

95

The monk was making for the nearby encampment, which consisted of circular, conelike tents of various sizes. The pennants on the larger ones were flapping in a gentle summer breeze, and suspended above their entrances were shields bearing coats of arms. The monk disappeared into one of the larger tents.

"That, at least, is a favorable concatenation of circumstances from our point of view," said Tjark.

"My dear Tjark," said Sir William, sounding slightly miffed, "would you be good enough to express yourself rather less obscurely?"

"By concatenation, Sir William," Tjark replied with a touch of eagerness, "I meant a fortunate coincidence or combination of circumstances. In this case, Enrico and Caruso's capture by a monk and the fact that this monk has just disappeared into the tent belonging to the person we're looking for."

"One moment." I shook my head to clear it. "Is that Cavaliere Goldoni's tent?"

"The coat of arms definitely indicates so."

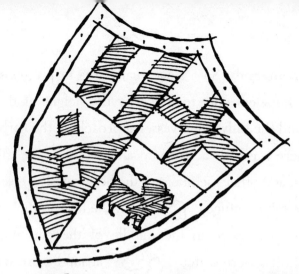

"Fine. **WHaT DO WE DO NOW?**"

"First I must analyze the situation."

Tjark fell silent and proceeded with his analysis.

The city walls loomed not far from the camp. They looked extraordinarily high and strong, and beyond them lay an expanse of very blue sea. A ship with a single sail was making for the city. It was low in the water, so it evidently carried a full cargo. That was all I could make out at long range.

I could, however, see that barriers of earth had been thrown up between the city and the camp, and that men armed with long spears were stationed on them at

97

regular intervals. So a siege really was in progress — a pretty hopeless one, to judge by the height of the city walls and the fully laden vessel approaching the harbor.

There was little activity in camp. Most of the knights, squires, and other members of the besieging force seemed to have taken refuge 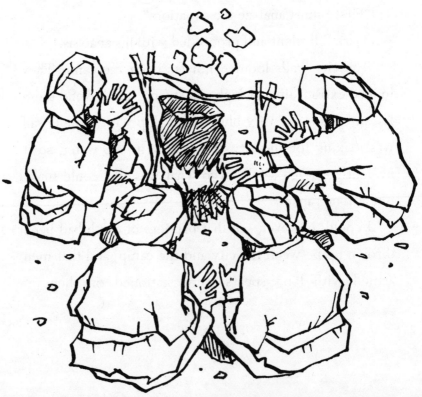 from the heat in their tents. In the open space in the middle of the encampment, several men were seated around a fire with an iron caldron simmering over it. Other men, who were wrenching twigs and leaves off some bushes on the edge of the camp, came over to the caldron and tossed them into it. **STRANGE.** What sort of brew were they concocting?

Tjark had completed his initial analysis. "I need more data," he announced. "There are two unknown factors that render it impossible for me to make a definite assessment of the situation."

"What unknown factors?" asked Sir William.

"The first is: How did the monk discover Enrico and Caruso? All this foliage provided them with excellent camouflage."

"Perhaps they nudged some branches at the wrong moment," I suggested. "Perhaps the monk spotted them moving."

"That possibility is exceedingly remote." Tjark's hovercraft propulsion unit started to emit a faint hiss. "In order to clarify unknown factor number one, I shall expand my data-collecting range." He was hovering now.

"You'd better not," I said. "You'll use up too much energy."

"The decision as to whether, when, and how I expend my energy supply," Tjark replied very condescendingly, "is mine alone." And he went hissing out into the open.

"What is unknown factor number two?" I yelled after him.

"My dear Freddy, can't you guess?" Sir William wagged his head at me. "You shouldn't allow outbursts of anger to cloud your thought processes."

For some reason, it seemed to have become fashionable to criticize my emotions. I thought hard. Unknown factor number two, unknown factor number two, unknown factor num . . . But of course! "Unknown factor number two," I said, "is why the monk grabbed them at all."

"Precisely." Sir William nodded. "What does he plan to do with them?"

"I can tell you that," said a voice from behind us.

I spun around.

aND THERE SHE WaS.

Her dark eyes were gazing at me.

Neat little ears, dainty pale pink nose, silky golden fur, and almost exactly the same size as me.

And that scent, that incomparable scent! I had never been privileged to smell it before, but I knew at once that this, and only this, was how a female hamster *ought* to smell.

She smiled. As she did so, her whiskers rode up a little higher on the left than the right. It made her smile look a trifle lopsided but utterly enchanting.

"Haven't you ever seen a female golden hamster before?" she asked, still smiling. "My name is Zuleika," she added.

Zuleika, yet! **ZULEiKa!** And what was my name? My name was Freddy, of course, as usual. "I'm Freddy," I said.

She nodded. "I know. And you're Sir William," she went on, turning to him. "I've been watching you both."

"May I ask why, my dear?" Sir William inquired in his most courtly tone.

"Do you imagine I wouldn't take precautions before venturing so close to an animal as big as you?" She gave another captivating smile. "Especially one with such big, sharp teeth?"

Sir William smirked and looked flattered. Then he said, "If I understood you correctly, you know what the monk has in mind for our two friends."

Zuleika looked grave. Very grave. That expression, too, suited her admirably.

Then she said, "HE INTENDS TO SLAUGHTER THEM."

CHAPTER SEVEN

I STARED AT ZULEIKA.

"Slaughter them? Slaughter Enrico and Caruso? You mean he plans to • • • **EaT THEM?**"

She nodded.

"But . . . why? I mean, why would he *eat* animals like them?"

Zuleika pointed to the camp. "Those men around the fire in the middle — why do you think they're stewing twigs and leaves?"

"No idea. . . ." Suddenly it dawned on me. "Surely they don't intend to eat them?"

She nodded again.

Sir William said, "Humans can't digest leaves and wood, even when they've been stewed. If those men eat them in spite of that, it means they're hungry."

"Not just hungry," said Zuleika, "they're on the verge of starvation. These Crusaders from distant lands have been encamped here for a long time. They've now reached the stage where they've eaten everything edible. There isn't so much as a peapod left for many miles around." She looked at us. "And then the monk discovers two animals, one of which, at least, looks very nourishing. Does that answer your question?"

"But we must do something right away!" Sir William had sprung to his feet. "They're in Cavaliere Goldoni's tent. We must rescue them!"

"Rescue them? From the Crusaders' clutches?" Zuleika shook her head dubiously. "That's a pretty tall order. At least wait till it's dark, or you'll all wind up in a cooking pot."

She went and peered through the overhanging branches, then beckoned me to her side. The fact that Enrico and Caruso were to be slaughtered in the near future

did not, I must confess, detract in the slightest from my appreciation of Zuleika's wonderful personal fragrance.

"Which is Cavaliere Goldoni's tent?" she asked. I pointed it out to her.

"Hmm," she said, "I don't see any smoke. It seems your friends aren't to be killed immediately. There must be a very good reason for that, so you can probably afford to wait until it gets dark."

SHE WAS RIGHT! I suddenly felt quite confident of rescuing Enrico and Caruso. I also felt extremely attracted to Zuleika. Beauty, personal fragrance, and intellectual ability — what more could the heart desire?

Zuleika withdrew into the shelter of our bush and I followed her. "Besides," she said, "the light is already fading. It'll very soon be nightfall. . . . Hey, what's that?" She sniffed the air. "What's that?" she repeated, her little pale pink nose twitching in the daintiest way. "What's that wonderful smell?" She turned around.

Tjark was standing just behind us.

He gazed at Zuleika.

Zuleika returned his gaze, still sniffing. After a while she said, "Freddy, won't you introduce me to your companion?"

I would tell her soon enough what my "companion" really was. For now I just said curtly, "Tjark, this is Zuleika."

"Zuleika . . ." Tjark drew himself up. "Zuleika! What a charming name — and how well it suits the person it belongs to!"

That bogus hamster was actually trying to hit on my Zuleika.

AND SHE WAS SMILING! She was treating him to one of those enchanting, slightly lopsided smiles that belonged to me alone.

"May I be so bold as to tell you," Tjark went on, "that your smile suits your face to a tee?"

That electronic bag of tricks evidently contained a very efficient chip designed for hitting on female hamsters. "Listen," I said, turning to Zuleika, "there's something I must —"

"I'm delighted," she said, "to make the acquaintance of a hamster who can express himself so elegantly — and whose personal aroma is so very pleasant. To be honest," she went on, "I've never come across such a scent before."

Of course you haven't, you delightful, unsuspecting creature. It was high time she learned the truth. "Listen, Zuleika," I began, but Sir William broke in.

"I think we can set off now," he said. "It's dark enough."

True. Okay, but shelving something didn't mean postponing it indefinitely.

"Then let's go rescue Enrico and Caruso," I said in a resolute tone, taking command. I hadn't the faintest idea how we would manage it, of course, but Zuleika might be marginally impressed. "Will we be seeing each other again?" I asked her.

"Why not?" She turned to Tjark. "I'd like to hear how you all get on, so I'll look in on you now and then." And she disappeared into the undergrowth.

Well, at least she'd said "you *all*," so she wasn't completely infatuated with that bogus hamster. "**LISTEN, YOU,**" I told him. "Keep your paws off Zuleika. She's mine, okay?"

"I see no logical reason why you should take precedence," he said, and added, "May the better hamster win."

"Better or worse doesn't come into it," I snarled. "It's a question of genuine or fake, you plastic phony. You're a machine, remember?"

"The expression 'plastic phony,' which you doubtless intended as an insult, is simply water off a duck's back where I'm concerned," Tjark said grandly. "Besides, I'm a machine equipped with everything that goes to make up a genuine hamster."

I was about to retort "That's just where you're wrong!" when Sir William stepped in again. **"ENOUGH!"** he commanded. "We've got a difficult task ahead — an operation requiring *teamwork,* so stop squabbling."

Night had fallen by the time we set off for the camp, I riding on the back of Sir William's neck, Tjark hissing faintly as he glided along leading us. It wasn't really dark, though.

"I've never seen such a night sky!" Sir William exclaimed. "Such an incredible number of stars, and so incredibly bright. How come, my dear Freddy?"

"Er, I guess it's because we're farther south, or something."

"You think so? Hmm . . ."

"The nearer one is to the equator," Tjark put in briskly, "the more stars one can see in the sky. Besides,

the atmosphere hasn't yet been polluted by gases and particles of dust, nor by the glow from brightly lit and densely populated areas."

Sir William whistled through his teeth. "Your general knowledge is truly remarkable, Tjark."

That isn't knowledge, Your Lordship, it's just stored information — just data from a data bank. If this bag of bytes doesn't have any data, he's lost. A computer is incapable of spontaneous ideas and flashes of inspiration.

"By the way, my dear fellow," Sir William went on, "have you worked out how the monk managed to spot Enrico and Caruso?"

"I've been unable to solve that problem, Sir William. I lack the data essential to a logical explanation."

GET iT, YOUR LORDSHiP?

"It doesn't matter," said Sir William. "Perhaps you'll have a flash of inspiration sometime."

No, he didn't get it. Why should he? Sir William had always treated Tjark like a living creature although he *knew* he was a machine. Zuleika *didn't* know that. I suddenly realized something: Putting her wise to Tjark was going to be a very tough job.

Silence reigned in camp. The men seated around the fires that flickered here and there among the tents were tightly wrapped in their cloaks. I suddenly noticed that the temperature had dropped, in fact it was almost cold. Strangely enough, though, I didn't *feel* cold. It *was* cold, but that was fine with me.

We had to make some minor detours around the fires to get to the tent with the Goldoni coat of arms. Sir William found the way there with ease, thanks to his feline eyesight, and Tjark glided purposefully along beside him. He seemed to have keener eyes than a hamster should.

I caught the sound of voices as we approached the tent. Several voices. Two men were talking together inside, sometimes interrupted by a third who spoke in loud, raucous tones.

"**HEAR THAT?**" said Sir William. He whispered the words, although no human could have picked up anything said in telepathic Interanimal.

"Of course," I replied, involuntarily whispering likewise.

"I hear it, too, but I can't yet catch what they're saying." Tjark spoke Interanimal at normal volume. He naturally saw no logical reason to whisper. "I'll translate as soon as I'm able to do so."

"Wait," Sir William whispered. "Follow me."

We tiptoed on until we reached the entrance. The canvas flaps that served as a door were the height of a man and firmly secured, but a reddish, fitful glow was issuing from a crack at ground level.

"Climb down, my friend," Sir William whispered, and I slid off his back.

We strained our ears. The voices were quite distinct now. The three men inside the tent were conversing in Old French, of course. Tjark glanced up at Sir William inquiringly. The tomcat whispered, "It's strange, I get the impression that there are only two men in there."

I listened intently. Sir William was right! There *were* only two of them, but one was speaking in two different voices alternately, one high-pitched and one low. The

113

other man, the one with the harsh voice, uttered a laugh from time to time. What was going on in there?

"Let's take a look," whispered Sir William. "I'll go first." Cautiously, he squeezed through the crack. Tjark and I slipped into the tent at his heels.

The first thing I noticed was a chest on the right of the entrance. It stood on four feet and was a couple of inches clear of the ground. In a pinch, I thought, I could hide beneath it.

The flickering reddish glow came from a torch in a sconce attached to the tent's central pole. Beneath it was a crude wooden table, and seated on a stool with his back to us was the fat little monk.

The other man sat facing him in a high-backed armchair. He had a jet-black beard and mustache and long, matted hair. Slanting across his forehead was a deep,

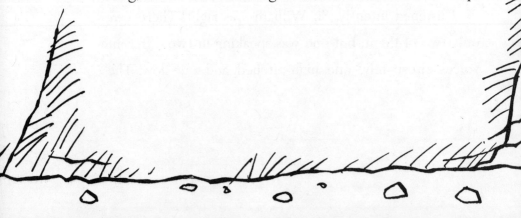

bloodred wound that had yet to heal. He wore a gray-green garment like a smock, plain and unadorned aside from the coat of arms emblazoned on his chest. They were the arms of the Goldoni family.

The knight was watching his companion expectantly. The monk said something in a high-pitched treble, then switched to a deep bass and said something else. He was the source of the two different voices. Whatever it was that he'd said, Cavaliere Goldoni uttered a loud, hoarse laugh and clapped his hands!

What was going on here?

AND WHERE WERE ENRICO AND CARUSO?

I cautiously shifted my position a little — and there they were. Enrico and Caruso were seated in the middle of the table doing something I couldn't at first identify. Then, all at once, I caught on: They were acknowledging the knight's applause by bowing!

What were they up to?

"*Frère Gros,*" Enrico exclaimed in Interanimal, "*j'ai terriblement faim!*" He spoke the words in a high-pitched voice, whereupon the tubby little monk cried out in an equally high-pitched voice, "*Frère Gros, j'ai terriblement*

faim!" He uttered the words after a moment's delay, almost like an echo.

"Frère Maigrichon," Caruso boomed in Interanimal, *"moi aussi, j'ai terriblement faim!"* A moment later: *"Frère Maigrichon, moi aussi, j'ai terriblement faim!"* the monk bellowed in a deep voice.

He was repeating what Enrico and Caruso had said. . . .

I sat there in a daze.

How was that possible?

How could the monk repeat what they were saying in Interanimal, like an echo?

Then I had a flash of inspiration — an idea that transfixed my brain like a thunderbolt.

The monk could *hear* Enrico and Caruso.

That was impossible, though. Humans couldn't do that.

But this person, the one seated at the table, could hear our telepathic language.

The potbellied little monk understood the language of animals!

117

CHaPTER EIGHT

"TJARK," SIR WILLIAM WHISPERED. "TRANSLATE, quick! But keep your voice down!"

"The monk or Enrico and Caruso?" Tjark whispered back. Why did he ask? Hadn't he realized that the monk understood Interanimal and was merely echoing what Enrico and Caruso said?

"All of them, of course. I want to know what they're saying." Sir William still hadn't caught on either, it seemed.

Enrico and Caruso were obviously playing the roles of monks. While they were addressing each other in *telepathic* Old French with the tubby little monk mimicking their voices in *human* Old French, Tjark telepathically translated what they were saying for the benefit of Sir William and me. To give him his due, he did so absolutely simultaneously.

"Brother Fatso," piped Enrico, "I'm not just hungry, I'm famished!"

118

"Brother Scrawny," boomed Caruso, "that makes two of us! I'd give my life for a nice, juicy steak!"

"Shall I tell you something, Brother Fatso?"

"Go ahead, Brother Scrawny."

"I'd give *your* life for a juicy steak."

Loud, hoarse laughter. Cavaliere Goldoni was tickled.

"You'd give my life for a juicy steak, Brother Scrawny?"

"You bet I would, Brother Fatso. **YOU'D MAKE A VERY JUICY STEAK.**"

More hoarse laughter.

"You mean you'd eat me?"

"That's right. One of us must sacrifice himself."

"But why me, Brother Scrawny, and not you?"

"Because I wouldn't make a juicy steak, Brother Fatso."

"That's true. You'd make a lousy steak."

"You can say that again. I'd never have the gall to serve you up a steak like me."

"Oh, Brother Scrawny, you're always so kind to me. . . ."

"Non, non, non!" The tubby little monk sprang to his feet. *"Non, Votre Excellence, non! Je ne peux pas répéter ce qu'ils disent!"*

Enrico and Caruso fell silent.

"Translate the monk's words," Sir William hissed. "And the knight's."

"NO, YOUR EXCELLENCY, NO!"

Tjark translated. "I can't repeat what they're saying!"

The knight's face had darkened. He ran his fingers

over the wound on his forehead. "Why can't you repeat what they're saying, Brother Francis?"

"Because monks would never speak in such a fashion."

"Don't you believe it, Francis. Simply pretend they're a pair of monks who have been lured to the Holy Land with false promises and are now starving."

Francis said nothing.

A sinister smile flitted across Goldoni's face. "But it's only a farce," he said. "A most amusing farce enacted by two most amusing little creatures."

"Oh, Excellency, please absolve me from having to repeat the *most* amusing words spoken by these *most* amusing little creatures. I find it too humiliating."

"But Francis, isn't humility a monk's supreme virtue? You want to be made a saint someday, don't you? Besides, may I remind you of something? You were the one that started repeating what they say.

You wanted to show me how well you understand the language of animals."

"Yes, Excellency, but only because you said, 'Those animals are making such eloquent gestures, it's as if they're trying to tell us something.' That's what induced me to translate for you." Francis suddenly lost his temper. "They're only playacting because they don't want to be slaughtered!" he cried.

"Very perceptive of you, little monk." The knight's face broke into another sinister smile. "They're playacting for their lives, that's why they're performing so well. They're preventing me from being bored, making me forget my empty belly. And the pain." Goldoni fingered his wound. "As soon as they cease to amuse me they'll be slaughtered for the pot. And now," he went on, leaning back in his chair, "let's continue. What was the last thing they said, Francis? Sit down again."

But Francis remained standing. "The last words were: 'Oh, Brother Scrawny, you're always—' " he broke off suddenly— " 'so kind to me.' "

Tjark. Tjark had completed Caruso's speech in Interanimal — aloud! How long had he been doing that?

"I knew it!" The monk spun around with surprising agility. "THERE! a CaT! a BiG TOMCaT!" He made a dash for Sir William.

Tjark disappeared through the crack like greased lightning and I raced after him. Sir William had gotten stuck halfway and was wriggling frantically. Freeing himself with a jerk, he shot out of the tent with the monk's hand in close pursuit. The hand was promptly withdrawn and its owner could be heard tugging at the fastenings inside.

Sir William lowered his head. "Get on, my friend." I did so. He straightened up and looked around. "Where's Tjark?"

The electronic hamster had disappeared. "Tjark!" called Sir William. No answer.

"We must get going, Sir William! That monk will be out in a moment."

Sir William sprinted off.

I'd been afraid that the monk would raise the alarm, but all remained quiet. Perhaps he thought that if he and Cavaliere Goldoni couldn't catch Sir William and have him for supper, no one else should. In any event, we had no difficulty in getting out of the camp and returning to our bush.

"I just don't understand why Tjark started speaking aloud," Sir William said on the way. "It can't have escaped him that the monk understands Interanimal."

Well, at least His Lordship had noticed that. I said, "Perhaps he assumed that the monk couldn't hear him over that conversation with Goldoni.

Let's hope nothing has happened to him and he finds his way back to the rendezvous."

He already had.

By the time Sir William dove under the bush with me on his back, Tjark was standing there as right as rain. With Zuleika.

That bogus hamster had seized the opportunity to make his move! However, his plan didn't seem to have been a total success. Zuleika was looking unmistakably standoffish.

I climbed down off Sir William, who promptly took Tjark to task. "Why did you disappear without waiting for us?"

"That's what Zuleika asked me." Tjark seemed faintly surprised. "There was nothing

I could do to help you. My first priority, therefore, was to get myself to a place of safety."

A perfectly correct assessment of the situation — for a logical-minded machine. Less so, it seemed, from a female hamster's point of view. Was it my imagination, or did the look on Zuleika's face say: "Fancy leaving his friends in the lurch! SHAME ON HIM!" Perhaps it wouldn't, after all, be too difficult to enlighten her on Tjark's true identity.

Just to rub it in, I asked him, "And why didn't you keep your voice down?"

"There was no need. Humans can't hear Interanimal, it's a law of nature. Mind you," he added, "my analysis of the situation conflicted with that assumption. However, I didn't have sufficient data to resolve that contradiction."

Quite so. For that he'd have needed a flash of inspiration, and computers never have them. After Tjark's declaration of mental bankruptcy, enlightening Zuleika about him would be child's play.

"My dear Tjark," said Sir William, "that monk can not

only hear Interanimal but *understand* it as well. What you call a law of nature isn't one at all. Exceptions to it obviously occur."

"May I store that information in my data bank, Sir William?"

"Please do." Sir William turned to me. "Freddy, what's your assessment of the situation?"

It looked pretty bleak. "Enrico and Caruso are in a bind," I said. "They can't jump down off that table, they'd break every bone in their bodies, so they'll have to go on playacting and being funny ad infinitum." On the other hand (this is just between us), hadn't those two comedians always wanted an opportunity to perform their skits in front of a human audience? "We've got to get them out, that's for sure," I went on. "The trouble is, I don't have the faintest idea how."

"Any suggestions?" Sir William surveyed us all. This meant, first, that he was just as devoid of ideas and, second, that he obviously didn't want to ask Tjark directly because the only animal present apart from us was —

127

"I'VE GOT a SUGGESTION,"

Zuleika said. "A pretty good one too."

"Er . . . Really, my dear?" said Sir William.

"Yes, really." Zuleika rose to her feet, looking extraordinarily attractive. Those neat little ears, those dark, expressive eyes, that little pale pink nose, that silky golden fur . . . But I guess I'm repeating myself. "As I see it," she said, "Enrico and Caruso can't be rescued by us animals. We must seek help from humans." And, on top of it all, that brainpower . . . One moment, though! There was something she couldn't possibly know.

"Seek help from humans? But how?"

"I've learned from Tjark that he can speak like a human."

"He *told* you that?"

"I could see no reason," said Tjark, "to keep it a secret from Zuleika."

128

I'LL BET YOU COULDN'T, YOU PLASTIC POPINJAY*!

Zuleika ignored his interjection. "At first I thought it was just an amusing trick," she said, "but now I think we should make use of it."

Where Tjark is concerned, Zuleika, that's precisely the right attitude to adopt.

"The only humans prepared to help us, if we can find any," she said, "will be enemies of the Crusaders. In other words, inhabitants of the city under siege."

"Sidon,"Tjark put in, "that's the city's name."

"You don't say!" Zuleika feigned surprise. "That's news to me." She still didn't realize that sarcasm was as lost on Tjark as it would have been on a rock. Never mind — his stock had fallen and mine was rising fast.

"Living in the city is a hakim, a physician skilled in the arts of healing. His name is Yakoub." Zuleika looked around at us. "You ought to ask Hakim Yakoub for help."

"Why him in particular, my dear?" Sir William inquired. "And may I ask who told you about him?"

"Nazira."

"I see. And who is Nazira?"

"She's a gerbil. A kind of desert rat with long hind legs."

"A rat, eh?" Sir William drawled, and I saw him lick his lips. It always made me feel a trifle uneasy when the predator in him surfaced, as it did from time to time. Being a civilized tomcat, however, he quickly regained control over his carnivorous instincts. "Well, well, so she's a gerbil," he said. "I assume from your description of Nazira that she gets around a lot."

Zuleika smiled. "She certainly does. Nazira knows everything that goes on in this area. A little while ago, two of the Crusader knights quarreled and attacked each

130

other with their swords. One of them was killed, the other so badly wounded that the rest of the knights thought he would die. They sought help from the townspeople."

"Why should the Crusaders have asked their enemies for help?"

Zuleika shrugged. "I don't understand it either."

"At this period," Tjark pontificated, "Western medicine was still in its infancy, whereas Asian medicine was very advanced. That being so, the Crusaders often sought the help of a hakim and granted him safe-conduct through their lines."

And now, you pompous machine, we'll see how wonderful your data bank really is. "Why should a hakim — an intelligent man — have agreed to help the enemy?" I asked.

"Because it gave him an opportunity to examine their camp."

HMMM. HE MIGHT HAVE A POINT.

"You know a great deal," Zuleika said to Tjark, "but why do you speak in the past? And why use strange words like 'medicine'?"

Those, Zuleika, are matters on which I shall enlighten you in the very near future.

Tjark was about to answer, but Zuleika had already turned away. "To make a long story short," she said, "the wounded knight owes his life to Hakim Yakoub."

"May I hazard a guess at the knight's identity?" I asked.

Zuleika gave me one of her enchanting, slightly lopsided smiles. "You may, Freddy."

"Why guess?" Tjark cut in. "The odds on his being Cavaliere Goldoni are ninety-nine to one."

Zuleika's smile vanished. She rolled her eyes in irritation.

TJARK'S STOCK HAD GONE BUST.

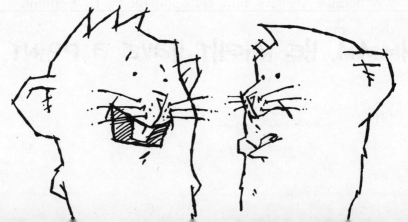

CHAPTER NINE

IT WAS ALL SETTLED.

After thorough discussion, we had decided that Sir
William, Tjark, and I would try to get into the city to see
Hakim Yakoub. How would we find our way to his house?
With the aid of the gerbil, of course. Nazira would guide
us there. How soon could we leave?

"As soon as I've met up with Nazira," said Zuleika. "She
looks in on me every night, so it won't be long before
she pays my burrow a visit." She turned to go, then
looked back at me and smiled. "SEE YOU LATER, FREDDY."

I returned her smile with
interest. "See you later, Zuleika."
Then she was gone.

Hard luck, Tjark. You think you know what
really matters, but you're wrong. What really
matters is the difference between genuine
and bogus. May the better hamster win.

133

Tjark drew himself up stiffly. "The so-called *genuine* hamster present may have forgotten, but *I* certainly have not: The purpose of our mission is to obtain some portion of Cavaliere Goldoni's anatomy, *not* to establish contact with female members of the hamster population."

Good heavens, Tjark. You've not only lost, you're a bad loser.

"My dear Tjark," said Sir William, "forget about our mission for the moment. All that matters at present is to rescue Enrico and Caruso."

Tjark didn't reply. He was clearly analyzing the situation. "You're right, Sir William," he said suddenly. "For the moment, Enrico and Caruso take priority. My conclusion: Instead of frittering away our time here, let's make a quick dash over to them. The monk and the knight may already be asleep. Then we can tell Enrico and Caruso, 'Don't worry, we're working on your case.'"

"Er, good idea, Tjark, my dear fellow."

All the way to Goldoni's tent and back? "Tjark," I said, "what about your energy reserves? How much time do we have left?"

"THIRTY-NINE HOURS, FORTY-TWO MINUTES, THIRTEEN SECONDS,"

Tjark replied promptly. A momentary pause, then: "That's less than my original estimate. It would be more sensible to remain here."

But then Enrico and Caruso would think we'd deserted them. . . . At that moment I had another flash of inspiration. "I suggest that only two of us go to lend Enrico and Caruso some moral support. You, Tjark, because you can understand Old French if the need arises, and you, Sir William, because you can transport Tjark on your back. No hovercraft propulsion means zero energy consumption."

"Freddy, old boy," said Sir William, "that's a positively brilliant idea. Climb on, Tjark." Tjark did so, and I

couldn't help feeling a little pang of envy to see him in my customary place on Sir William's back. There wouldn't have been room for both of us, though — Sir William was big, but not that big. He and Tjark left the shelter of the bush and disappeared into the gloom.

There I sat, all on my —

"Oh, all on your own?"

It was Zuleika.

"Where are your friends?" she asked.

I told her, and she nodded. "Friends must stand by one another. Still, it's a shame Tjark isn't here. He smells so good."

"Zuleika, there's something I must tell you about Tjark. He's —"

"— a pain in the neck, I know, but he smells simply divine."

Tjark's stock *hadn't* gone bust after all. That scent of his . . . How did she account for it? No golden hamster had ever smelled like that. And how on earth did she account for the sudden appearance of the five of us?

"I'd like to ask you something, Zuleika. What do you make of us? A big predator, two funny rodents, and a pair of hamsters suddenly appear out of nowhere. Where do you think we sprang from?"

"I ask you! That's obvious."

"Er, really?"

"You escaped from a showman who exhibited you as curiosities."

CURIOSITIES, EH? Great. She was right, though. We were a curious-looking bunch. I ought to leave it at the showman version, I told myself — she won't believe the real story anyway — but I had to ruin Tjark's prospects once and for all.

"Zuleika, don't you wonder why Tjark doesn't smell like a golden hamster?"

She shook her head. "He may look like you and me, but he isn't a *golden* hamster. He belongs to another breed of hamsters, I don't know which."

It was all going like clockwork. "I'll now let you in on a secret, Zuleika: Tjark isn't a hamster at all — he isn't even an animal." I paused for effect. Then I said, "He's an artificial creature."

Zuleika stared at me. "aRTiFiCiaL . . . ?"

"Yes, he's a machine. A kind of contraption or apparatus. How can I put it . . . ?" I relapsed into silence.

Zuleika's eyes flashed. They really did. I mean, it's easy enough to say or write that, but now I witnessed the phenomenon at first hand. Zuleika's dark eyes not only flashed, they bombarded me with thunderbolts. Deadly ones, what's more.

"It hasn't escaped me, Freddy," she said, "that you and Tjark have been competing for my affections. You weren't doing badly either, but *now* what have you done?"

No idea, but I felt sure she'd tell me.

"You've just tried to eliminate your rival from the contest in the most unsporting manner. Tjark an artificial creature? Why not have done with it and tell me he comes from another world?" More thunderbolts. "That was really mean of you, Master Freddy!" She turned away, then added over her shoulder, "You can tell your companions that Nazira the gerbil will be here shortly." And she disappeared.

There I sat, all alone and feeling lonely.

Very lonely.

Not only lonely but sick at heart.

And who was to blame? Tjark, the artificial hamster, who had the gall to make a play for Zuleika in spite of his artificiality, which stank. As if there were a genuine possibility that he and

Zuleika could ever be an item like two genuine hamsters!

But Zuleika thought he was genuine. And, when you came down to it, she could hardly do otherwise.

It took me a while, but I managed it in the end. I had no choice: I would treat Tjark like a fellow hamster.

From now on it would be a question not of genuine or bogus, but of who was the better of us.

And now, my dear Tjark, I said to myself, you can show how effective your hitting-on-female-hamsters chip really is.

Sir William and Tjark were back in an alarmingly short space of time. "**WHAT'S WRONG?**" I asked. "How are Enrico and Caruso?"

"There's good news and bad," said Sir William. "The good news is, the monk and the knight had dozed off, so we could speak with them. The bad news is, they'll soon have to resume their performance."

"They're utterly exhausted," said Tjark. "Their brains are going addled. It won't be long before they run out of ideas."

Was that possible? Couldn't those two comedians dream up any more stupid antics?

"They hope they'll be able to keep it up tomorrow," Sir William said, "but the fact remains, the sooner we get them down off that table the better. *If* we can manage it at all," he added gloomily. He looked around. "That gerbil — hasn't she put in an appearance yet?"

"Nazira, that's my name," said a voice from outside our bush.

"HERE I aM, NaZiRa THE GERBIL REPORTING FOR DUTY!"

And she sprang through the overhanging branches in a single movement.

One thing soon became clear: Nazira was probably the most fidgety rodent in the whole of the East (not to mention the West).

She had dainty little forepaws and big, muscular hind legs. Her forepaws she used to clean her whiskers incessantly; her hind legs propelled her just as incessantly to and fro. Okay, so she sometimes stood still for several seconds at a time, but an instant later **—WHOOSH—** she would be somewhere else. If Sir William had been overcome by one of his predatorial impulses, Nazira would have driven him to despair.

"Quick, quick, quick!" she panted. "You want to go to Hakim Yakoub's house? Nazira knows the way there and how to get inside." **WHOOSH!** She landed in front of Sir William. "You're big, you are — very, very big." **WHOOSH!** She landed behind him. "Black as night, too, very black. No problem, no problem." **WHOOSH!** She landed right in front of me. "And my reward, my reward? No reward, none at all. Happy to be here. Happiness is a long trip into the city."

"Listen, Nazira," I said, "you'll have to make some allowances for us. We aren't quite as fast as — "

WHOOSH! She landed in front of Tjark. "Around and around and around," she said breathlessly. "I'll circle you as we go, it'll make the trip seem even longer."

"You're an unusual creature," said Tjark. "You're transmitting such a dense series of signals, my input channel is completely choked with them."

"Gentlemen," Sir William cut in, "I think we'd better simply set off before I get dizzy."

Which we did.

This time I traveled in my usual place on the back of Sir William's neck while Tjark glided along beside us with a faint hiss. I told them that Zuleika thought we'd escaped from a showman's menagerie.

"Hardly my own choice of a career," said Sir William, "but I'm sure Enrico and Caruso would take it as a compliment."

Nazira circled us the whole time, as she'd promised. At least, I assume she did because we never saw her unless we paused, uncertain of our route. Then she would reappear like magic and point us in the right direction.

We had no problem moving over the terrain and getting past the armed sentries, who stood leaning on their long spears beside flickering campfires.

But then we reached the city walls.

They towered into the sky overhead.

How were we ever to get over them?

I must have uttered the words aloud, because Nazira repeated them impatiently.

"GET OVER THEM? GET OVER THEM? NONSENSE!"

she panted. "That's a human approach to the problem." She bounded to and fro in front us. "*Infiltrating* them, that's the answer for creatures our size. We'll *infiltrate* them." She leaped into the air and landed in front of Sir William. "You're big — very big — but black as well, black as night. It might work, it just might."

"Are you expecting trouble?" I asked.

Nazira landed beside me. "Trouble . . . ?" All at once she broke off and sat quite still. Then she said, "The people in the city are afraid of desert rats. They're distant relations of mine and never harm a soul, but the people in the city hunt them. Not in order to eat them, so why? Perhaps because there are so many of them. If we're spotted, they may mistake us for desert rats." Nazira leaped into the air suddenly. "Follow me, follow me," she hissed. "Follow me closely and we'll make it, we'll make it." And she sped off.

Sir William went bounding after her, but it was all he could do to keep up. Tjark, on the other hand, seemed to be keeping up with ease. However, I dreaded to think of the drain on his energy reserves by the time this operation was over.

We flitted along the foot of the towering city walls. I had once seen a book containing pictures of medieval European cities whose walls were enclosed by moats filled with water. There was no moat here, perhaps because the walls were far higher and stronger — so high that no moat was necessary — or because water was scarce. At any event, we raced along the foot of the walls without meeting any obstacles. Nazira came to a sudden halt. "This is the place," she whispered. "This is where we get into the city."

Looming above the wall was a huge tower. A gate tower, to be precise, because I now caught sight of the portcullis: a grating constructed of heavy, ironclad beams that formed an impenetrable barrier. Impenetrable for humans but not for animals. We slipped through it. Inside a fire was burning in the gateway, and beside it stood two men armed with pikes.

"WE CAN RISK IT NOW, LET'S GO!"

Nazira set off at her usual breakneck pace, and Sir William and Tjark raced after her. We flitted past a slumbering sentry and into the city itself.

I had read in the book containing pictures of medieval European cities that their narrow streets were very primitive, being unpaved and having no sidewalks. The mounds of garbage in the alleyways naturally attracted vast numbers of rats, which in turn spread the plague.

Sidon's paved streets and sidewalks were so clean, they might just have been swept by a whole fleet of municipal sanitation trucks.

"Watch out for patrols!" Nazira hissed. "They go looking for desert rats. If a patrol appears" — she came to an abrupt halt beside an opening in the edge of the sidewalk — "dive into a drain hole."

"**a DRAiN HOLE?**" said Sir William.

"The Asian cities of this period," Tjark cut in, "had sophisticated drainage systems for discharging rainwater."

"Rainwater?" I scoffed. "In this arid region? My dear Tjark, it's time you gave your data bank an update."

"In this part of the world," Tjark insisted, "the rainfall between November and March can amount to four hundred millimeters, or roughly fifteen and three-quarter inches."

"Really?" Sir William shook his head in amazement. "INCREDIBLE!"

He had no idea how much rain 400 millimeters represented, of course. Neither did I, but I knew — or rather, I suddenly sensed — that it rained here in the winter. Pretty heavily too. Hamsters scarcely noticed this, however, because they were hibernating. They lay in their nice, dry nests and dreamed of grain and pine kernels. And beetles . . . Beetles . . . ? What kind of beetles? I had never seen a live beetle in my life, still less eaten one. . . . But I knew once again — no, I sensed — that beetles were the tops. Nourishing and extremely tasty. They were far more delicious, even, than mealworms. . . .

I must have been daydreaming, because I suddenly heard Nazira whisper, "Here we are."

We had ended up in an alleyway — a dead end, as far as I could tell, and it skirted the high city wall. We halted outside a small, inconspicuous door. "Hakim Yakoub's house," said Nazira. "This is the back door. How do you get in? That's for you to discover."

"But didn't you say you knew how to get inside?" I was wide awake now.

"I said I knew where the entrances were. This is one of them."

Fine, so it was a misunderstanding, but how would we get into the house? Nazira raised her little forepaws in a gesture of regret. "The front door's locked and the courtyard wall is too high. You mustn't try to get in through that drainpipe either." She pointed to a dark hole at the foot of the wall. "It's roomy enough, but there's a grating on the inside. Against rats." She straightened up. "Lots of luck," she said, and

WHOOSH — she disappeared.

"What a fidgety creature." Sir William grinned. "At least she thoroughly updated my knowledge of rodents." He lowered his head. "I think you should get off now, Freddy." I slid to the ground. "Well, gentlemen, how do you suggest we proceed?"

That was a genuinely Sir Williamish question. Tjark answered it as follows: "In view of our limited scope for maneuver, Sir William, I suggest we have some tea while waiting." Was I wrong, or had Tjark winked at me?

Sir William sighed. "I suppose we've no choice. . . ." Suddenly he raised his head and pricked his ears. "There's someone coming."

I could also hear footsteps now, and they were drawing nearer.

"The law of probabilities," Tjark said, rather hurriedly, "suggests that a patrol is approaching."

Sure enough, the patrol was turning into our alleyway. It consisted of two night watchmen, one carrying a lantern and a spear, the other something that looked like a bundle on a pole. It was a net. A net for catching things in! The men were coming toward us — they would spot us at any moment. Where to?

VE WERE iN a DEAD END.

"Quick, Freddy, climb on! I'll try to dart between their legs."

"Too risky," Tjark said quickly. "I recommend that hole in the wall."

OF COURSE! I dove into the drainpipe with Tjark hissing at my heels and Sir William bringing up the rear.

Then one of the watchmen shouted something!

"There! There goes one!" Tjark translated. "After it!"

Sir William shot into the drainpipe just as we heard the two men break into a run.

CHAPTER TEN

THE COURTYARD WALL MUST HAVE BEEN PRETTY thick, because the drainpipe that ran through it turned out to be a regular tunnel.

A tunnel with only one exit, unfortunately.

I scampered to the far end at once, and there, as Nazira had predicted, access to the courtyard was barred by an anti-rat grating. It was woven out of thick strands of steel wire, and the mesh was so fine that there was no point in me and Tjark trying to squeeze through it, let alone Sir William. On the right-hand side I noticed some hinges, on the left a sliding bolt. The grating could evidently be opened. At present, of course, it was firmly secured.

The entrance at the street end went dark: One of the watchmen was peering in. "I can't see that confounded rat," he said (Tjark provided us with a simultaneous translation), "but it's well and truly trapped. Did you see what a plump beast it was? We'll get it, never fear."

His head disappeared. "But take care it doesn't give us the slip."

"A bit big for a rat, wasn't it?" said the other man. "You really think it was one?"

"What else could it be? Anyway, we'll soon see."

"They can't get at us in here," Sir William whispered. "Their arms aren't long enough."

No, but they had a long . . . With a clattering sound, the spear was thrust into the drainpipe. The steel tip crept toward us, probing in all directions, and whenever it grated against the masonry that lined the walls the harsh sound bored into my ears. I couldn't make out the tip itself, but Sir William, with his tomcat's glowing green eyes, could see it clearly. He pressed up against the wall with the fur on his neck bristling furiously, but that

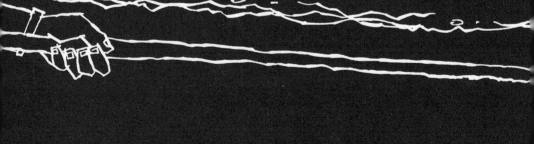

wouldn't do him much good. His body almost filled the tunnel, so it wouldn't be long before the sharp point stabbed him. . . .

From behind me came another clatter — no, it was more of a rattle. I spun around to find two eyes —HUMAN EYES— peering through the grating. Then the eyes disappeared and the bolt was drawn. The grating swung back on its creaking hinges and we darted out into the open air.

I heard the grating close again and turned to look. Beside it, visible in the light of a lantern suspended from a bracket on the wall of the house, crouched a girl. Around ten years old, with a mop of dark, curly hair, she was wearing a green-and-gold embroidered gown. And then her scent came wafting toward me: a breathtaking fragrance of jasmine.

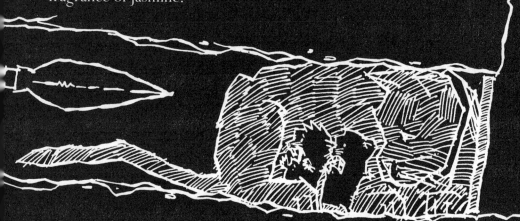

"In my opinion," said Tjark, "that was what is commonly termed a close call."

"My dear fellow," said Sir William, "I share your opinion one hundred percent." The fur on his neck had almost settled by now. "But we mustn't forget our good manners. Would you kindly introduce us to our youthful benefactor, and assure her that we . . ."

From outside in the street came the sound of loud knocking. It grew louder still, and the night watchmen started shouting. "OPEN UP!" Tjark translated. "OPEN THIS DOOR! OPEN IT AT ONCE!"

A woman's voice issued from the house, the quavering voice of an old woman. "I'm coming, I'm coming!" We heard a bolt being drawn. The back door flew open with a crash, the old woman uttered a cry of alarm, and the watchmen came storming into the courtyard, the one with the spear in the lead. "That rat! Where is it?!" he yelled.

"And who opened the grating?" shouted the one with the net.

The girl had risen to her feet. She was slender and not very tall for her age, but she stood there in her long gown and said calmly, "It was me. I opened the grating."

"That's forbidden! Rat gratings must be kept shut."

"Where is it?" The man with the spear looked around wildly. "Where's the rat that ran in here?"

"The rat?" The girl folded her arms. "No rat ran in here." She pointed to Sir William. "It was our pet cat."

The two men stared at Sir William.

"He was out hunting rats. I just let him in again."

"Hmm," said the man with the net. "And the grating's shut." He turned to his companion. "I told you it was too big for a rat. What now?"

But the man with the spear didn't reply. He was pointing to me and Tjark. "**THERE! WHAT ARE THEY?**"

"They're my pet golden hamsters." The girl crouched down. "Hey, you two, come here."

"I think we can afford to risk it," Tjark said to me.

"What's your own assessment of the dangers inherent in our present situation?" But I'd already set off. I needed no second invitation to inhale the scent of jasmine at close quarters.

"Oh well," said the man with the net, "I guess we'd better go."

"Durdana," the girl said, "would you please show the gentlemen out?"

"With pleasure, Atira." The old woman, who was evidently a servant, beckoned to the two night watchmen and disappeared into the house with them.

"Tjark, old fellow," said Sir William, "would you introduce us now? But please do it tactfully," he added, "so you don't frighten the girl."

Tjark nodded. He rose on his haunches in front of Atira, and . . .

But first I must explain something: Although Tjark spoke Old Arabic with Atira, I could understand what they were saying because he simultaneously (!) translated it into Interanimal. Tjark was the tops — at least as far as his language chips went. I couldn't wait to see if he also contained a tactfulness chip. . . .

So Tjark said to Atira in Old Arabic, "Mistress, please don't be alarmed. I'm not a jinni or evil spirit of some other kind; I'm simply Tjark, the talking hamster. The three of us have escaped from a showman's menagerie. My companions can't speak, but they can understand what you say." He indicated us in turn. "This is Freddy, and this is Sir William. We hamsters, and Sir William in particular, owe you a heartfelt debt of gratitude for rescuing us." Tjark spread his paws wide and bowed. "Mistress, we lay our devotion at your feet."

Tjark not only contained a tactfulness chip; he also possessed a bamboozling-Atira chip.

SHE WAS CAPTIVATED. "What a handsome little fellow you are! And they call you Tjark? That sounds like the name of an intrepid warrior. I'm sure you must be the leader of your band."

Sir William and I exchanged glances.

Atira turned to us. "So you're called Sir William? That sounds mature and dignified. And you're Freddy. What a funny name! You must be the comedian of the trio."

"Take it easy, old boy." Sir William smirked at me. "Don't be miffed."

WaS I MIFFED? Of course I was. After all, I was Freddy the unique, the author of four books. I'd taken a fancy to Atira, so I was far from indifferent to what she thought of me. Besides, there was her breathtaking scent of jasmine. . . . On the other hand, my book-writing counted for nothing here.

"Oh," Atira exclaimed, "but I haven't introduced myself yet." She rose to her feet. "I'm Atira, the daughter of Yakoub, the hakim."

"Delighted to make your acquaintance," said Tjark, every inch the leader of our little band. "I can now reveal, mistress, that we came to present your father with a request."

Atira nodded. "So you aren't here by chance. I guessed as much right away."

I mentally clasped my brow at that. Atira had been suddenly confronted by a big tomcat and two hamsters, one of which not only possessed the power of speech but had requested permission to ask her father something — and she seemed to think it all quite normal. Still, I told myself, weren't we in the Land of the Thousand and One Nights?

"You'll be able to speak with my father," Atira said, "but he's out at present. Until he gets back . . . Oh, but I'm sure you must be hungry." She clapped her hands. "Durdana!" she called. "WE HaVE GUESTS!"

A half hour later we were sitting with Atira in the "Fountain Room," as she called it. And indeed, a little fountain was splashing into a basin facing the doorway, which had a carpet suspended over it instead of a curtain. Candles were burning in sconces on the walls. Atira had seated herself on a shelflike bench that ran around the walls and was covered with carpets and cushions. We ourselves were sitting on a rug on the floor.

164

(It looked pretty expensive, and if Enrico and Caruso had been with us, we might have had a problem.) We were feeling well-fed and thoroughly contented — discounting the fact that our "Rescuing Enrico and Caruso from the clutches of Cavaliere Goldoni" operation wasn't exactly making lightning progress.

The food had been excellent. A piece of mutton for Sir William and some pine kernels, carob beans, and prunes for Tjark and me. Tjark had skillfully pretended to eat, although the nourishment *he* required was unobtainable here. I hadn't asked him how much time we had left. His answer wouldn't have made any difference to the situation, and besides, I was counting on him to let us know if things became really tight.

Before Durdana brought our food, Atira had said, "There's no need for her to know that you can speak, Tjark. Anything *she* overhears the entire neighborhood knows within hours, and I think my father should hear it first."

But Hakim Yakoub took his time. After a while, Atira turned to Tjark and said, "Can't you tell me what it is you want to ask him?"

"With pleasure," he replied. "Two of our companions have been —"

"Tjark!" Sir William cut in sharply. "I forbid you take any independent initiatives. You must discuss things with us first."

"But I only wanted to —" Tjark protested in Interanimal.

"DO I MAKE MYSELF CLEAR?"

Sir William bared his enormous fangs.

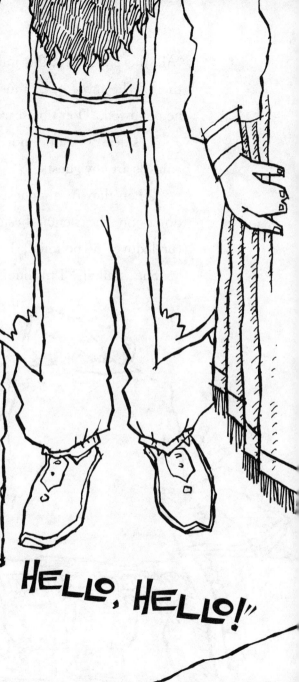

"Perfectly." Tjark relapsed into silence.

Atira looked from one to the other. She had noticed that something was wrong but, being tactful by nature, she didn't press the point.

An uneasy silence prevailed.

At long last the carpet over the entrance was thrust aside and Hakim Yakoub appeared. A great big giant of a man with a huge black beard, he filled the whole doorway. "HELLO, HELLO, HELLO!" he roared.

167

"Ah, there they are, the animals. Durdana told me about them." The three of us must have given a jump, because he bellowed, "Don't be scared, I won't hurt you."

"I sincerely hope not, Father," said Atira. "These animals are my guests."

"Then they're my guests too," Yakoub roared. He sat down on the bench beside his daughter. "Atira, my turtledove," he boomed, "how are you?"

She smiled. "I'm fine, but I'd feel even better if my dearest father kept his voice down a little."

"Very well, I'll only whisper from now on," Yakoub whispered. He turned in our direction. "I do whatever my daughter tells me," he added hoarsely. "She rules the roost here, that's why."

"Honestly, Father," said Atira. "You shouldn't make such jokes in front of visitors. Our guests might believe them."

"The animals, you mean?" Yakoub looked first at her and then at us. "You mean they can understand what we say?"

"Every word of it."

"Is that so?"

Hakim Yakoub gazed at us in silence for quite a while. Then, slowly, he began to nod. "I suspected as much. The fact is, I've always known that animals can understand us human beings. But how did *you* know, my turtledove? You seem quite sure of it."

"I am." Atira pointed to Tjark. "This golden hamster can not only understand us, he can speak as well."

"HE CAN SPEAK?!"

169

"It's true, noble sir," squeaked Tjark. "Mine is a skill possessed by only a select handful of animals."

Sir William and I couldn't help exchanging another glance.

"You can really speak?" asked Yakoub. "Not like those gaudy African birds that can be taught to repeat things mechanically?"

"I speak with intelligence and understanding. If you'll permit me, sir, I'll act as your interpreter."

"Then I shall be able to converse with you animals!" Yakoub threw up his hands in delight. "To think that I should live to see this day!"

"You were almost denied that pleasure, dearest Father." Atira looked at him gravely. "Your rat catchers were hot on our visitors' heels. They very nearly killed them."

"**MY RAT CATCHERS?**" Yakoub shook his massive, bearded head indignantly. "Please choose your words more carefully, my turtledove. Those rat catchers were appointed by the city council, as you know. At my suggestion, it's true, because I know what havoc the

170

plague can cause. I've experienced it firsthand." He turned to us. "I apologize if you were made to fear for your lives, but the desert rats that stray here from far-off India carry fleas in their fur, and those fleas can transmit the plague to human beings. If plague breaks out in a beleaguered city where numerous people live crowded together in a small space, that's the end of the city's population. And that," he concluded, turning back to Atira, "is why they're *my* rat catchers."

Atira bowed her head. "I'm sorry, Father."

"My turtledove." Yakoub gazed at her fondly. "So you encountered these animals by chance?"

She shook her head. "Not by chance. They came here on purpose — they want to ask you something."

"To ask me something? I can't wait to hear what it is."

Tjark glanced at Sir William, who told him, "Let's not rush things, my dear fellow. To begin with, simply inform the worthy doctor that our request has something to do with the Crusaders encamped outside the city."

Tjark did so. "The Crusaders, eh?" said Yakoub.

"That's interesting. I've just come from a meeting of the city council at which one of our secret informants reported some curious goings-on in their camp."

"a SECRET iNFORMANT?" I asked, and Tjark translated.

"Well, yes. We've bribed some of their servants — even some of their squires — and they tell us what the Crusaders are up to. We don't want any unpleasant surprises, do we?"

I nodded. "These curious goings-on — what form do they take?"

"One of the knights is behaving oddly. His name is Goldoni."

We looked at one another.

"Goldoni has clearly gone mad," Yakoub went on. "I'm not surprised, incidentally, but more on that later. Anyway, there's a monk accompanying the Crusader army, and it seems Goldoni has been compelling the unfortunate man to entertain him with foolish tricks of some kind."

"And the other knights tolerate his behavior?" I asked.

"Yes. The monk isn't too popular with them, so they're glad he's being made to play the fool. Added to which, they're reluctant to cross swords with Goldoni. It's been unwise to tangle with him since he was wounded in a duel."

We all nodded.

"You knew of this?"

"We animals have our own secret informants," Sir William said smugly. "The duel was witnessed by an inquisitive gerbil. We also know that you, Master Yakoub, healed the knight in question."

Yakoub shook his head. "Healed is an exaggeration, the wound was very deep. Goldoni has probably developed gangrene — he must be out of his mind with pain."

"He's in pain all right," I confirmed. "He often clasps his head."

"YOU'VE SEEN HIM?"

"We have indeed," said Sir William. "Worthy Hakim,

this is the moment at which we should like to present our request. May we do so?"

Yakoub nodded.

"Freddy, my friend, would you take over?"

I struck a pose. "Hakim Yakoub," I began, "we're really a band of five animals who escaped from a showman's menagerie, but two of our number have fallen into Goldoni's hands." I went on to report that Enrico and Caruso had been captured by Brother Francis and

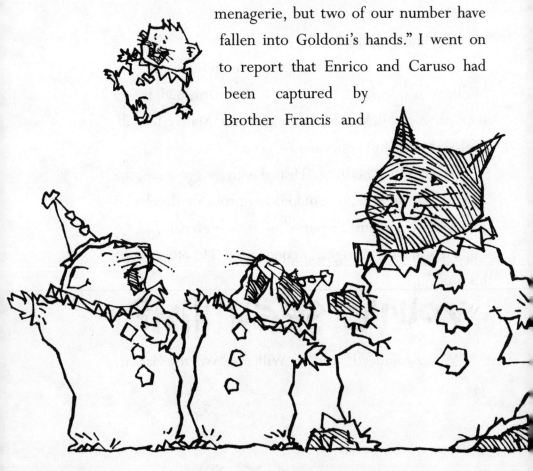

described how they were playacting for their lives in the knight's tent.

"And the monk genuinely understands the language of animals?" Yakoub asked.

"He does."

Yakoub, heaved a sigh. Then he asked, "These companions of yours — what kind of animals are they?"

"They're rodents that bear a vague resemblance to miniature pigs," I explained. "They come from . . ." I remembered just in time that South America hadn't been discovered yet. "They come from somewhere far across the sea. They're known as guinea pigs."

Yakoub looked at all three of us in turn. "Unless I'm much mistaken, you want me to persuade Goldoni to release these guinea pigs. Am I right?"

It was all going splendidly. "That's what our request boils down to, yes."

"Any idea how I'm to manage it?"

175

"Well, yes. You saved Goldoni's life, so we thought he might be grateful enough to **. . . NO?"**

Yakoub had shaken his head. "If I expected him to be grateful, he'd be mortally offended. Then he wouldn't have to be grateful to me anymore, do you understand?"

I didn't, to be honest, but this was 850 years ago. So now, how were we to engineer the guinea pigs' release?

"I have an idea," said Atira.

"What is it?"

"We'll ransom the guinea pigs for food. Goldoni would

be bound to let them go in exchange for a generous supply of food."

"He certainly would." Yakoub gazed at his daughter with pride. "My clever little turtledove! That could be the solution."

I was now feeling pretty relieved after all. Although the cheerful giant had gained my trust at once, I'd never expected him to grant our request so readily. So quickly too. If we maintained this speed, Tjark's reserves of energy would be more than sufficient for our purposes.

"That could be the solution," Yakoub said again, tugging at his huge beard, "if it weren't for one little obstacle." He fell silent, still tugging away.

"Obstacle, Father?" Atira asked. "WHAT OBSTACLE?"

Yakoub let go of his beard, but he still didn't speak. At length he said, "It's no use."

What was no use, pray?

"It's no use," Yakoub repeated. He surveyed us sadly, shaking his head. "I won't be able to rescue your two companions."

177

CHAPTER ELEVEN

I FELT AS IF SOMEONE HAD EMPTIED a pitcher of icy water over me.

Even as he uttered the words, I realized that he had weighed them with care. His decision was final.

We could expect no help from Hakim Yakoub.

Atira was incredulous. "But, Father," she exclaimed, "surely you can't be serious! It would mean certain death for those two guinea pigs!"

Yakoub didn't speak for a while. Then he said, "You must believe me, Atira, and I hope you animals will also accept that I've made this decision with a heavy heart. Permit me to explain."

The Crusaders hadn't invited him to pay their camp another visit, he said, so he couldn't expect safe-conduct. On the contrary. "The Crusaders regard us as their enemies, so they'd take me prisoner on the spot. They might release me in return for a

ransom. Then again, they might not. They might even kill me." He looked at us. "I hope you don't think I'm afraid of dying" — I honestly didn't — "but I'm responsible for my motherless daughter, who would then be an orphan, and also for the inhabitants of this city. I'm the only doctor here who knows how to combat the plague."

"But, Father," Atira persisted, "you could say you wanted to dress the knight's wound. He'd protect you if you visited him as a doctor."

Yakoub shook his head. "I couldn't rely on that. Although Goldoni told me I could always count on him, a wound like his can change a man. It can make him vicious and spiteful. Believe me, my turtledove, I know what I'm talking about."

Sir William looked at me. "The hakim's decision is final — I imagine we're all agreed on that?" I nodded, and he turned to Tjark. "My dear fellow, be kind enough to tell Master Yakoub the following: We thank him for having listened so readily to our request, and we understand his reasons."

179

Tjark passed this on. "I thank you in turn for appreciating my position," said Yakoub. He sighed. "Unfortunately, that doesn't help your companions." He got to his feet. "You're welcome to remain our guests for as long as you wish, needless to say. Good night, and the best of good fortune." He walked to the door, thrust the length of carpet aside, and disappeared.

Atira had also stood up. "That *can't* be his final word on the subject," she said. "There *must* be some solution. I'll have a word with him. Wait here for me." And she followed her father out.

"Well, my friends," said Sir William, "we're dependent on ourselves again. What do we do now? Any ideas?"

 **"TWENTY-THREE HOURS, TWELVE MINUTES, FORTY SECONDS,"** Tjark said suddenly. "That's how much time we've got left."

"What?! Is that all?" I said. "Why didn't you say so before?"

"I consumed a large amount of energy on the way here, but I'd been counting on Hakim Yakoub to carry me back. My energy reserves would then have looked far more favorable."

"Great," I said. "Under existing circumstances, how will they look by the time we get back to the Crusaders' camp?"

"I'll have barely seven hours left."

Seven hours . . . Only seven . . . **WHaT a DiSaSTER!**

Seven hours' worth of energy would probably be insufficient even to get Tjark from the camp to the bush, our point of departure for the future.

My fur had started to bristle in panic, I noticed. I quelled that physical reaction with difficulty.

"I could transport you back to the camp one after the other," Sir William said, thinking aloud.

"That would drastically increase the risk of our being caught and killed by rat catchers," Tjark declared. "By six hundred percent, give or take a little."

"Then we'll have to take the bull by the horns," I said. "We get back to Goldoni's tent as fast as possible, Sir William stretches out beside the table to act as a mattress, and Enrico and Caruso jump down."

"I predict that Enrico and Caruso won't jump."

"They *will*, they don't have any choice!"

Tjark shook his head. "They can't, they're programmed not to. Even when scared to death, no guinea pig can bring itself to jump off the edge of a table."

"All right, all right!" The fur on Sir William's back was also starting to bristle. "Then I'll leap onto the table and push them off. Perhaps we can find something soft for them to land on."

"Whatever we do," I said, "we must do it before the knight is overcome with hunger."

"CLIMB ON, FREDDY!" Sir William bellowed. "QUICK!"

I clambered onto his neck and sank my teeth in his fur.

At that moment Atira reappeared. Very slender and not very tall, she stood there and calmly surveyed us in turn. "Don't panic," she said. "I've got the answer."

"You mean your father has had an idea?" said Tjark.

She shook her head. "*I've* had an idea. I'll tell you what it is later — Father's waiting for me. First I'll take you down to the cellar, then I'll tell my father you've disappeared and I'm going to bed. When everyone's asleep I'll come and join you."

"And then?" I asked.

"Trust me. It won't be the first time I've done it."

What hadn't she done for the first time?"

"Come on." She took one of the candles from the wall.

"Mistress," said Tjark, "I'm rather tired. Could you please carry me?"

"Of course." Atira picked him up with care and put him on her shoulder. "Let's go, but keep quiet." She tiptoed out of the room with Sir William padding softly after her.

We made our way across the courtyard, then through a low archway and down the cellar steps. Ahead of us lay a long passage with doors leading off it on either side. Atira went to the far end of the passage, where she pointed to a niche in the wall. I saw a circular grating.

"The cellar drain," she whispered. "It slopes downward."

The drain was just wide enough to admit a human child. A very slim one.

"I'll guide you out," Atira said, "and take you to Cavaliere Goldoni."

We sat beside the grating and waited. I soon started to itch all over, the way I always do when condemned to inactivity and compelled to stay put. I felt like racing around the cellar, but Atira had taken the candle with her and blundering around unknown territory in the dark would have been reckless on my part. And, in our predicament, irresponsible.

I wasn't exactly reassured by the nervous, tigerish way Sir William kept pacing to and fro, his green eyes glowing.

Tjark, on the other hand, was tranquillity itself. He had switched over to his energy-saving mode — a kind of hibernation for electronic hamsters.

At last, after nearly two hours, we heard someone tiptoeing down the cellar steps. Then a human figure came into view, holding a candle in its outstretched hand. Yes, it was Atira — the scent of jasmine was unmistakable — but in other respects . . .

She'd blackened her face, presumably with soot, and had exchanged her long gown for a tight-fitting dark gray jacket buttoned up to her chin. The rest of her outfit comprised ankle-length trousers, a pair of sandals, and a cloth wound around her head like a turban. She was carrying a bag with a cord attached to it.

"I couldn't come before," she whispered. "Father went on pacing up and down his bedroom for ages." She put the bag down and stuck the candle to the floor with melted wax. Then she unbolted the grating and swung it open. "This drain leads beneath the city wall and comes out in our garden."

"Is that what you've done before?" I asked her. Tjark, who had promptly switched to full power, translated for me. "Crawled out through the drain, I mean?"

She nodded. "Yes, with some friends of mine. That was before the Crusaders came. We could still play outside the city walls in those days." She crouched down. "Now listen. Plan number one: We crawl out and sneak into the Crusaders' camp."

OKAY, BUT WHAT THEN?

"Then we creep into Goldoni's tent. If he and the

monk are asleep I'll pick up your companions and we'll simply steal out again."

Easier said than done. I glanced at Sir William, who shrugged. "We've no choice," he said.

"There's an eighty-percent chance," Tjark announced, "that plan number one will fail."

"What if the knight and the monk *aren't* asleep?" I asked Atira.

"If they aren't, we switch to plan number two." She patted the bag. "Dried meat, white bread, salt, butter. Understand, all of you?"

"Seventy percent," said Tjark.

"We have no choice," Sir William repeated. "And if we dillydally here much longer, there'll be nothing left of Enrico and Caruso but a heap of gnawed bones."

"The trouble is, plan number two suffers from a major drawback." Atira eyed us gloomily. "I don't speak the Crusaders' language."

"That's the least of our problems, mistress," said Tjark. "I'll interpret for you."

"You speak their language?" Atira beamed at him. "I might have known it. No wonder you're the leader."

"Now listen, Atira," I cut in, "Tjark isn't —"

"FREDDY! ARE YOU OUT OF YOUR MIND?!

Sir William's eyes glowed even greener than usual. "Tjark, would you inform Atira that we'd like to leave at once?"

Tjark transmitted the message and Atira nodded. "I've got a safe place for you," she told him, picking him up and putting him on her head. "Hide inside my turban," she said. Tjark disappeared from view completely. "Right, let's go." She blew out the candle. "We won't need a light; it's straight ahead all the way."

She took hold of the cord attached to the bag and crawled into the opening, towing the bag behind her.

Sir William lowered his head. "On you go, Freddy."

It was a good half hour later when I dismounted from Sir William's back. We had reached the entrance to Cavaliere Goldoni's tent.

The first part of our operation — crawling under the city wall by way of the drain, which was dry and surprisingly clean, then sneaking past the sentries into the Crusaders' camp — had gone as smoothly as Atira had expected or, rather, hoped. We were now confronted by the part for which Tjark had predicted an eighty-percent risk of failure.

No torch was alight inside the tent; only a faint red glow issued from the crack beneath the flaps, which were secured. "Embers are preserved overnight in an iron basket," Tjark whispered in Interanimal. "Kindling a fire from scratch was an extremely laborious task in those days." He was forever lecturing us, but I guess he simply couldn't restrain himself, being a walking data bank.

I strained my ears. Deep breathing and faint snores could be heard: Goldoni and Brother Francis really were asleep. Perhaps we were in luck — perhaps the second part of our operation would go as Atira hoped. I could detect no sound from Enrico and Caruso. They were probably asleep too — wisely so.

Cautiously, Sir William thrust his head through the crack. "In we go," he whispered after a while, and

189

disappeared. Atira undid the lowest knot, eased the flaps apart, and squeezed into the tent with Tjark still concealed inside her turban. Once she had pulled the bag of food in after her, I followed.

The chest was still in its place beside the entrance. Facing it was the table flanked by the stool and Goldoni's chair with the fire basket glowing in the background. Where was the knight himself? Over there against the side of the tent, only dimly visible. He seemed to be lying on a kind of crudely constructed cot. He was the source of the deep breathing. The monk, snoring gently,

was asleep on a straw pallet on the other side of the tent.

The glow from the embers didn't reach the tabletop, which lay in shadow, so Enrico and Caruso could not be seen.

"Take cover beneath the table," Sir William said softly. Tjark transmitted the message to Atira in a low voice and we darted across the tent.

"We mustn't startle Enrico and Caruso," Sir William whispered, "or they might squeak. I'll jump up on the table, wake them, and explain what we have in mind. Then Atira can fetch them down from there."

And then we would sneak out again. I was gradually beginning to believe in our chances of success. Tjark passed the word to Atira, who nodded.

Sir William crept out from beneath the table, braced himself, and leaped into the air. He landed without a sound.

I listened.

Nothing.

Why didn't he say something? Go on, I thought, wake the pair of them!

Suddenly a silent shadow materialized beside us: Sir William had jumped down again. "They're gone," he whispered.

"Gone? What do you mean?"

"ENRICO AND CARUSO AREN'T THERE ANYMORE."

CHaPTER TWELVE

IT TOOK A MOMENT TO SINK IN. . . .

We'd gotten there too late!

Goldoni's hunger had prevailed over his sense of humor. Goldoni had . . .

"Is the table bare?" Tjark inquired. "I mean, did you spot any, er, leftovers?"

"No," Sir William whispered. "Besides, we'd smell it if Goldoni had stewed or roasted them."

Of course! I very nearly let out a squeak of relief. But where were they?

Sir William looked around. "We can't search the tent. There's no other choice; we'll have to call them. Would you do it, Tjark? I suspect they're more likely to respond to your voice than mine. But keep it down, please."

"Enrico?" Tjark called in a penetrating whisper — in Interanimal, of course. "Caruso?"

Silence except for the monk's snores.

"Enrico?" Tjark called in a low voice. "Caruso?"

Still no response. Just a loud snore from the monk.

"Enrico?" Tjark shouted. "Caruso?

WHERE aRE YOU?"

And then, over a very loud snore from the monk, we heard, "**HERE! IN THE** cHEST! In the big chest beside the entrance!" That was Enrico's voice. "It isn't locked," Caruso chimed in, "but the lid's too heavy for us to lift!"

"Don't worry, we'll soon get you out!" Tjark called in Interanimal.

Sir William reached the chest in two mighty bounds. I set off too. Just as I did so, I heard Tjark whisper, "Mistress,

the guinea pigs are in the big chest over there!" Atira darted after us, crouching low.

She straightened up, reached for the lid, and . . . **FOOTSTEPS!** Hurried human footsteps!

Sir William sneaked behind the chest in a flash, and I dove out of sight beneath it.

I could see Atira's little, sandal-shod feet. They were suddenly confronted by another pair of sandal-shod feet, but the feet were big and calloused and the sandals scuffed and worn.

"Oh!" cried Atira.

"Your Excellency!" the monk called. Then he said something I didn't understand. Tjark had stopped translating.

All at once the gloom was dispelled. I darted to the end of the chest and peeked around one of its feet. Goldoni was standing beside the fire basket. He had kindled a torch. Brother Francis was gripping Atira by the arm.

"Well, well," said Goldoni, "a little lad. Or . . . no, you look more like a girl." But why could I understand him? Caruso was translating him into Interanimal! What on earth was he thinking of? The monk, who understood our language, would know at once that some other animals had gotten into the tent. . . .

No, that was nonsense, he must have heard us long ago. He'd been woken by Tjark's cries and pretended to go on snoring.

"Your Excellency," said Francis (simultaneously translated by Enrico), "this girl must have broken into the tent accompanied by an animal of some kind."

Just then, Tjark poked his head out of Atira's turban. "That's me, Your Excellency," he said in Old French, not forgetting to translate for our benefit.

Goldoni stuck the torch in the bracket on the central tent pole and came over to the monk. He ran his hand over the wound on his forehead. "Brother Francis," he said,

197

"the Holy Land is beginning to grow on me. First two funny little animals that keep me entertained, and now one I can talk with." He turned to Tjark. "I wonder what you're going to say to me."

"If you'll permit me, most gracious sir, I'll begin by passing on a suggestion from my mistress. She'll say it in her own language, and I, with your permission, will translate it into yours."

Goldoni nodded. "Permission granted. Well?" he said to Atira. "What's this suggestion of yours? Who are you anyway?"

"I'm Atira, the daughter of Hakim Yakoub."

"Yakoub's daughter, eh? Fancy that!" The knight smiled grimly. "To what do I owe the honor of a visit at this late hour?"

"I've come," Atira said firmly, "because I . . ."

And here I simply must break off and mention something I couldn't mention before, such was the speed with which events had been developing. This is that Atira not only smelled of jasmine but was courageous and self-possessed to a positively admirable degree. Mind you, I couldn't quite discount the possibility that she'd failed to grasp the full extent of the danger she was in. To be honest, however, the same applied to me. . . .

So she said in a firm voice, "I've come, Cavaliere Goldoni, to make a bargain with you."

a BARGAIN? Well, well. What manner of bargain?"

"Release the two animals in the chest, and I'll give you that." She pointed to the bag, which was still lying beneath the table.

"Brother Francis," said Goldoni, "see what it contains."

Francis let go of Atira and hurried over to the table. Atira was now free. If need be, she could have reached the mouth of the tent in two strides and disappeared. But there was no need: Brother Francis was smiling broadly. He had detached the cord from the bag and peeked inside, and his round face had lit up like the full moon emerging from behind a cloud.

He went over to Goldoni and showed him the contents of the bag. The knight bent over, cupping a hand behind his ear, and the monk proceeded to whisper something.

Tjark, still ensconced in Atira's turban, pricked up his ears but offered no translation; Francis was whispering too softly.

Goldoni listened intently, and it seemed to me that the bloodred wound on his forehead was starting to glow.

The knight nodded abruptly and straightened up. He gave Atira a thoroughly amiable smile and said, "Atira — that was your name, wasn't it? Well, Atira, daughter of Hakim Yakoub, about your offer . . . Oh, how discourteous of me, do sit down." He indicated the stool beside the table.

After a moment's hesitation, Atira went over to the stool and sat down.

"This meat, bread, and butter you're offering would undoubtedly be a fair exchange — *if* those two funny little animals were all I had to bargain with. But as luck would have it . . ."

All at once, with surprising agility, Brother Francis

darted over to Atira with the rope and swiftly lashed her ankles to the legs of the stool.

"... I now have something else to barter, don't I? Hakim Yakoub's daughter, to be precise. I'm sure you'll agree with me when I say that I'll get more for her. A great deal more."

aT THaT MOMENT TJaRK JUMPED.

He jumped out of Atira's turban — had he gone mad? — and fell like a stone. When he was only a paw's-breadth above the ground, there was a hiss so loud that the humans must have heard it too. He zoomed across the tent, shot through the crack between the flaps, and disappeared into the night.

Brother Francis had sprung to his feet, but Goldoni made a dismissive gesture and said something I didn't understand.

Cautiously, I backed away to where Sir William was standing. He jerked his head at the mouth of the tent and we darted outside. Then he lowered his head, I jumped on, and he bounded off.

Tjark was waiting beneath our bush.

So was someone else.

Zuleika was sitting there too — Zuleika, with her dainty little ears, her dark, expressive eyes, her little pale pink nose, her silky golden fur, and that incomparable scent of . . . Okay, okay, enough said, but there she was. The few inches between her and Tjark might have been a mile, she was looking so unapproachable.

"Well," she said, "was this another occasion on which your companion could do nothing to help you? Was it his first priority, yet again, to get to a place of safety?" She didn't deign even to glance at Tjark.

He eyed her unhappily. Then he looked at me.

"Tjark acted with great deliberation and exceptional

presence of mind," I told her. "Things aren't what they seem, Zuleika."

She stared at me suspiciously. "Is this some new trick of yours?" she demanded. "I mean, springing to his defense like this?"

"I can't explain now. The situation . . ." I broke off. I really couldn't explain the situation, not at this stage. "But believe me. . . ."

"Hey, you two," said Sir William, "I'm far from averse to listening to squabbles between the sexes, but this is hardly the time for it." He looked from me to Tjark and back. "After this latest development, what do you think we should do?"

Tjark glanced at me. "Sir William, only one conclusion can be drawn, even from a very superficial analysis of the status quo: We must alert Hakim Yakoub."

Sir William nodded. "Yes indeed. I myself have gained the same impression."

"So it's back to the city as fast as possible," I said.

"SIXTEEN HOURS, TWELVE MINUTES, FIVE SECONDS,"

said Tjark.

"What?! Why so little?" I asked.

"It was extremely energy-consuming, breaking that fall to the ground. I'll never make it to the city and back again."

Zuleika gave a sarcastic smile. "So Master Tjark can't make it, eh?"

"Zuleika," I said, "things really aren't the way you think they are." Now I would *have* to explain the situation. "Hakim Yakoub's daughter is in Goldoni's clutches, and —"

"His daughter? Goldoni has captured her?"

"Yes. That's why —"

"Then you must go to the city come what may. 'I'll never make it' simply won't do."

I could only raise my paws helplessly.

204

Zuleika smiled at me. She looked at me with that enchanting, slightly lopsided smile of hers. "I must say, Freddy, I think it's very decent of you to —"

"Forgive me, my dear, but time presses." Sir William turned to me. "There's only one solution, my dear Freddy: I transport Tjark to the city and you wait here. Agreed?"

I nodded.

"Very well, then. On you get, Tjark!"

But Tjark was sitting there stiffly with his ears pricked. "There's something going on," he said.

I could hear it now too: A babble of voices was drifting over from the Crusaders' camp.

Tjark was listening closely. From the look of it, he had boosted his hearing to its highest degree of sensitivity. "That voice pattern — I've got it on file." He listened some more. "He's speaking Old French, but it's him all right. The probability ratio stands at ninety-eight percent."

"WHO'S HIM?"

Tjark listened a while longer. Then he said, "One hundred percent. Hakim Yakoub is in the Crusaders' camp."

CHAPTER THIRTEEN

I WAS SITTING BENEATH THE BUSH whose overhanging branches screened us from the outside world.

I was sitting beneath the bush with Zuleika.

Sir William had set off with Tjark. Not to the city, of course, but to Goldoni's tent. It was clear that Hakim Yakoub had discovered Atira's disappearance and guessed where she had gone.

"In my estimation," Sir William had said, "if the hakim manages to free his daughter, he'll certainly be able to do something for Enrico and Caruso."

"The probability of that is thirty percent," had been Tjark's estimation.

"Hardly a cause for rejoicing," Sir William had conceded, "but better than zero, no? When I think of getting stuck here!" Sir William shook himself like a wet dog. "I'd never survive it."

WOULD I SURVIVE IT? You bet I would. I would not

206

only survive;
I would make
my home in
these natural
surroundings,
which might have
been created especially
for an animal like me. . . .

"On you go, then, Tjark," said Sir William.

Tjark's reserves of energy had to be conserved — that, too, was clear. Who could tell what lay in store for us? Whatever happened, we had to have enough energy for the return journey.

"As soon as the situation allows, old boy, I'll come and give you a lift to the tent." And Sir William and Tjark had vanished into the darkness.

"So that's how you do it," Zuleika said. "I wondered, of course, how you and Tjark would make it all the way to the city." She thought for a moment. "He's odd. Why does he count off the hours? And what hours is he counting?

They've got nothing to do with the time of day." She looked at me as if I ought to make some comment.

I was not going to start on about "artificial creatures" again; it would only put me back in her bad books, but I had to say *something.* Then I had an idea. "Tjark has set himself a deadline for the release of our friends." I shrugged. "It's a whim of his. He has one or two like that."

Zuleika nodded. "You told me he was an artificial creature."

I stared at her. Had she noticed something?

"You were only kidding, of course." She smiled. "But I forgive you." Then, she said seriously, "But he isn't a hamster either. Neither a golden hamster nor any other kind."

"Er, really? How did you arrive at that idea?"

"It was like this: He was sitting with his back to me when I got here, so he couldn't see me coming and he didn't hear me either. But he ought to have *smelled* me."

She thought for a moment. "I mean, I don't expect him to go berserk when he smells me, but he didn't react at all. He didn't smell *a thing*. It was really creepy, because there isn't a hamster alive that can't smell *anything*."

That was true. But if Tjark wasn't a hamster, what was he? She was bound to ask me. I racked my brains.

"And you know what?" she went on. "There's something fishy about his personal aroma as well. All right, so it's wonderfully fragrant, but it's not real — like one of those perfumes humans make. Does Tjark drench himself in perfume? Why would he do that?"

WHY INDEED? I racked my brains some more.

"Oh well," Zuleika said suddenly, "it doesn't matter. He's just a fairground freak, that's all. Not my type." She gave me one of her enchanting, slightly lopsided smiles. "Why were *you* in the showman's troupe? I mean, what tricks can *you* perform?"

What tricks indeed? I thought feverishly.

Zuleika was regarding me with an expectant air.

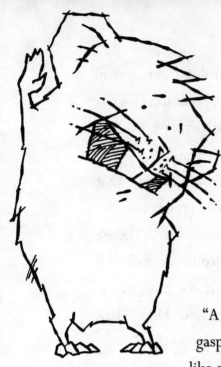

And then, quite instinctively, as if in response to a command, I sat up on my haunches like a dog begging and raised my right forepaw. I raised it as high as I could. And then . . . I waved it at her.

And Zuleika fell over.

She doubled up with laughter.

She lay there shaking with mirth. "A golden hamster that can wave!" she gasped. "A golden hamster that can wave like a human!

WHaT a HooT!"

And she went on laughing. She shed no tears — only humans shed tears when they're amused — but she couldn't help roaring with laughter.

I sat there on my haunches, watching Zuleika laugh, and suddenly I could see myself through her eyes. I saw myself sitting there with one paw in the air — saw myself waving.

And, like her, I couldn't help roaring with laughter.

"How did you wind up in a menagerie?" Zuleika asked me later.

"I was born in one," I told her. It was true, in a way.

"You were born in captivity?"

That was absolutely true. I nodded.

"How awful!" she exclaimed. "You mean it wasn't until after you escaped that you found out what it was like to live in the wild?"

I nodded again. "My home until then was a cage." No, that was nonsense. It sounded as if I'd languished

in a
dungeon
like the Count of
Monte Cristo. But
could I tell her about my
cage in Mr. John's apartment?
About my comfortable nest, my well-
stocked larder, my jungle gym? She
wouldn't understand what I was talking about.

"It was a very comfortable cage," I said. "It might
have been made for a golden hamster."

"*Made* for a golden hamster?" she protested.

"No golden Hamster belongs iN a Cage!"

I shrugged and left it at that.

"Then you've never been in a golden hamster's
burrow?"

"Never," I said. I'd only been in a burrow belonging to
some field hamsters. It was a maze of incredibly wide
tunnels and vast underground chambers. I'd felt like a

212

human who'd strayed into a world inhabited by giants. "No," I said, "I've never been in a golden hamster's burrow."

Zuleika hesitated. Then she said, "Would you like me to show you mine?"

Alone with Zuleika in her burrow . . . I realized in a flash that I'd never get a second chance. I would never again be able to visit a golden hamster's burrow. In my world, the modern world, nearly all golden hamsters lived in cages. There might be a handful of them living in the wild, but where and how many no one could say. Millions of golden hamsters lived in cages, and none of those cages — of that I felt sure — was big enough and, more important, contained enough earth for its occupant to dig a burrow. However, I was naturally familiar with the layout of a burrow; that knowledge is imprinted on our genes. "I should very much like to see your burrow," I said.

"Very well." She looked at me. "You know the rules: The female hamster is boss. All right?"

"ALL RIGHT."

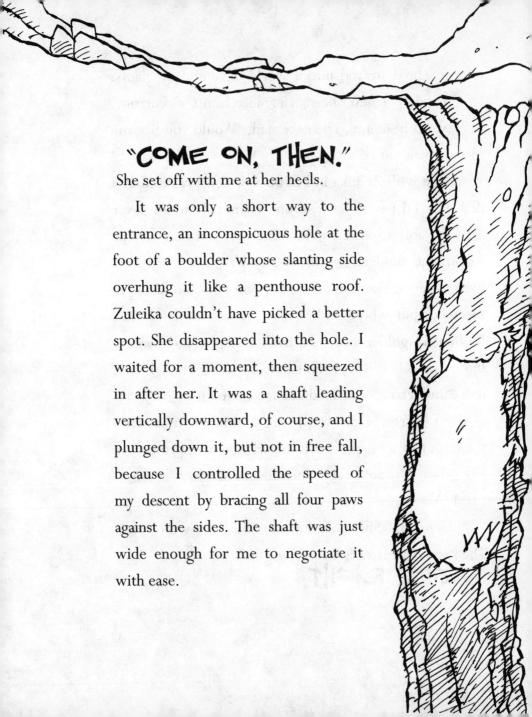

"COME ON, THEN."

She set off with me at her heels.

It was only a short way to the entrance, an inconspicuous hole at the foot of a boulder whose slanting side overhung it like a penthouse roof. Zuleika couldn't have picked a better spot. She disappeared into the hole. I waited for a moment, then squeezed in after her. It was a shaft leading vertically downward, of course, and I plunged down it, but not in free fall, because I controlled the speed of my descent by bracing all four paws against the sides. The shaft was just wide enough for me to negotiate it with ease.

The same applied to the horizontal tunnel in which I landed, which was a perfect fit. Zuleika was waiting for me. She beckoned me with a jerk of the head and led the way.

Following her, I suddenly became aware that I could **SEE**. Although little of the brilliant starlight outside penetrated the burrow, I had a very clear and distinct image in my head. My nose could **"SEE"** Zuleika's scent and that of the soil surrounding us. My whiskers, which probed every little clod of earth, every pebble, could **"SEE"** the tunnel walls, and my ears could **"SEE"** Zuleika walking ahead of me. I'd always known, of course, that golden hamsters didn't **SEE** with their eyes alone, but I'd never been as conscious of it as I was now, while following Zuleika along the tunnel.

If we continued to walk straight ahead, this tunnel would sometime slope upward and end in a camouflaged exit. I was as certain of this as if I'd excavated the burrow myself. But branching off halfway along would be the main tunnel leading to the larder. Before that, on the right, would come a short passage leading to the bathroom and, on the left, a longer one that ended in the sleeping chamber.

"I'm sure you know what a burrow ought to look like." Zuleika had paused at the entrance to the main tunnel. "But knowing isn't everything." She looked at me. "How are you feeling?"

I didn't have to think twice or search for words. "I feel good," I said. "as if i've come home."

She nodded.

There was no need for me to add that her burrow could never be my real home. Hamsters live on their own. They're loners by nature.

"You need a burrow yourself," she said. "A hamster without a burrow is like a plant without roots." She paused. Then she added abruptly, "You could dig one nearby. The ground here is very suitable, so think it over." She turned and squeezed into the main tunnel. "First I'll show you my larder," she went on as I followed her along it. The entrances to the sleeping chamber and the bathroom were not immediately opposite each other but slightly offset in the proper way.

The larder smelled of wheat and pine kernels. Zuleika's stores were on the meager side, which rather surprised me. "I still have plenty of time," she said. "It's going to be a long summer — the winter rains will be late this year." How did she know that? Simply because any hamster living in the wild knows such things by instinct.

I, on the other hand, couldn't be expected to know them. I'd arrived only yesterday at noon, with the others. . . .

"Zuleika," I said, "don't be offended, but Sir William may be waiting under the bush outside, and, er . . ."

She nodded. "Of course, your two companions must be rescued, that's the most important consideration at present. But . . ." She broke off. "However things turn

out, you'll be needing a place to live, so think it over."
She smiled. "I reckon the two of us could be good
neighbors."

We could, Zuleika. We could indeed — *if* I didn't
have to return to another world. . . .

We got back to the bush to find that Sir William
wasn't there yet.

"A pity." said Zuleika, "I'd like to have shown you my
sleeping chamber. Still, you must know what such places
look like." She treated me to one of her enchanting,
slightly lopsided smiles. I gazed at her dainty little ears,
her . . . Okay, okay.

But there she was, looking at me.

I LOOKED BACK AT HER.

"Freddy," she said softly.

"Yes?"

She raised her right forepaw, but only fractionally.
Then she made an economical little gesture: She was
beckoning me closer. Slowly, I moved toward her.

We sat down facing each other.

And then I felt her whiskers brush mine.

MY FUR STOOD ON END.

For the first time in my life, my fur was bristling with
delight. . . .

Chapter Fourteen

SIR WILLIAM APPEARED SOON AFTERWARD.

"Quick, my dear fellow, the hakim is just being taken to see Goldoni. Climb on, please."

I did so. "See you later, Zuleika."

"See you later, Freddy," she said with a smile.

Sir William sped off. He raced through the starlit night. Although dawn was already breaking, I felt sure we wouldn't be spotted in spite of the paling sky. Sir William knew exactly where the sentries were posted, and he also knew the location of all the best bits of cover. After all, this was the sixth time he'd covered the route between our bush and Goldoni's tent.

Tjark was waiting for us outside the entrance. "The knight has dismissed the sentries who escorted the hakim

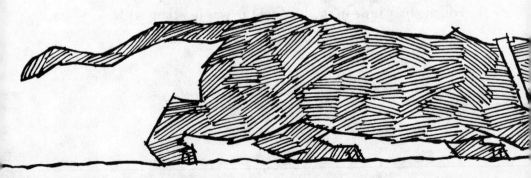

here," he whispered, "and the hakim has just been inquiring about his wound. Nothing else has happened."

"Then let's go in, my friends," Sir William said in a low voice. "You two creep beneath the chest and I'll hide behind it. And please don't take any risks. Don't try to contact Enrico and Caruso for the time being, or the monk may detect our presence."

WE CREPT INTO THE TENT.

Goldoni was seated in the armchair, his wound glowing red in the torchlight. He was toying with a dagger lying on the table in front of him. Brother Francis was standing beside the stool on which Atira was sitting, her ankles still tied to the legs. She was gazing up at her father, wide-eyed with anxiety.

The hakim had stationed himself in front of the table. A tall, stout figure with a big black beard, he looked utterly calm and serene. A number of small leather pouches were suspended from the broad belt he wore over his hooded cloak.

"Well, well," Goldoni was saying (Tjark translated for us), "so you think my wound is paining me?"

"I don't think so," Hakim Yakoub replied. "I can see it is."

"Shall I let you into a secret, Hakim? Your eyes don't deceive you." Goldoni smiled grimly. "But I'll tend the wound myself. I don't need your help."

"With all due respect, it would be unwise of you to dispense with my services."

"Who says I'm dispensing with your services?" Goldoni's smile turned nasty. "You're going to render me a very, very great service." He turned to the monk. "You've had some practice at this, Brother Francis. Proceed."

The monk gave a broad grin. "If the worthy hakim would come and stand here?" He pointed to the central tent pole.

Yakoub hesitated.

"COME, HAKIM." Goldoni picked up his dagger. "Surely you don't want your daughter to come to any harm?"

Yakoub stationed himself with his back against the pole.

The monk, who had fetched some rope from the corner of the tent, tied him to it carefully and securely.

"You once told me that I could always count on you. Is this what you meant?" Yakoub demanded. "Is this all it's worth, your word of honor as a knight?"

"A knight will eat his word of honor in a pinch." Goldoni replaced the dagger on the table. "Let's see how much your city council will pay for a hakim — a very valuable hakim," he added. "The only one in town with a knowledge of the plague."

Yakoub stared at him.

223

"Don't look so astonished, worthy Hakim. We, too, have our secret informants." Gingerly, Goldoni felt the wound on his forehead. "At all events, your city councillors will receive a proposal from me before the day is out." He touched the wound again. "My terms will be pretty stiff, but they'll meet them if they're wise. Then they'll get you back — with your daughter thrown in."

Goldoni suddenly winced. He turned to Brother Francis and yelled, "Those funny little animals — go and get them! **AT ONCE!**"

Francis hurried over to the chest.

I darted back just as the monk's big, sandaled feet appeared in front of me. He lifted the lid of the chest. Enrico and Caruso made no sound as he picked them up. They had probably been awake and listening for ages, so they were prepared for this eventuality. Francis carried them over to the table.

I must admit I felt genuinely touched to see them again after so long — or at least, it seemed like a long time, although it could only have been eighteen hours at the most. The monk put them down, and there they sat. Enrico looked very small to me — even scrawnier than usual — and Caruso appeared to have lost a lot of weight in eighteen hours. He made an almost slender impression.

"GET ON WITH IT, YOU FUNNY LITTLE CREATURES!"

Goldoni barked at them. "And woe betide you if you don't make me laugh! You'll disappear into my belly quicker than you can squeak."

Enrico bowed to him. "Your Excellency," he said. Tjark simultaneously translated the words into Interanimal for our benefit, and Francis loudly repeated them in Old French an instant later. "With your permission, Excellency, I shall enact the role of Enrica, the wife of a knight who's away at the Crusades."

"And I," Caruso said, bowing, "will — likewise with your permission — play Sir Caruso."

Oh dear, surely they weren't going to —

"What you are about to see, Excellency, is incredibly amusing."

225

"I hope so," Goldoni said grimly, "for your sake."

Enrico struck a pose and declaimed in a high-pitched voice:

"On the battlements I tarry, yearning for my love's embrace."

Oh dear, oh dear, Enrico and Caruso were falling back on one of their old skits. They'd run out of ideas — they were exhausted. Still, perhaps Goldoni would be amused nonetheless.

Caruso, who had retreated to the other side of the table, came hurrying over.

"Swiftly to thy side, Enrica, filled with eagerness I race."

Goldoni clutched his forehead, but neither of them noticed.

"Ah, with passion all atremble," Enrico warbled, *"I await my heart's desire."*

Goldoni's face darkened. . . . Stop it, you guys, don't go on!

Sir Caruso raised both paws in a theatrical gesture.

"I am likewise drunk with passion. Let me in, my blood's on fire!"

"THAT'S ENOUGH!" Goldoni yelled.

Enrico and Caruso gave a jump.

"How dare you, you impudent creatures?" Goldoni demanded in a menacing whisper. His voice rose to a shout again. "A knight's wife would never be unfaithful to her husband! Never!" He seized the dagger. "Brother Francis! Light a fire under the cooking pot!"

"Cavaliere Goldoni!" cried Hakim Yakoub, tightly bound to the tent pole but erect and unafraid. "Stop, Cavaliere Goldoni! Let the animals live!"

"Why should I?"

"Because your pain is more intense than your hunger — far more intense. These animals will serve no purpose inside your belly. They won't relieve your pain in there. You spurned my assistance. At least accept theirs."

Goldoni suddenly grinned. "Know something, Hakim? You'd have made a good preacher. Very well." He turned to Enrico and Caruso. "I'll give you one last chance," he said grimly. "If you don't make me laugh again, I'll slaughter you." To Yakoub: "Not because I'm hungry, but because killing you would relieve my pain. So get on with it!" he shouted at Enrico and Caruso.

And Enrico and Caruso did so. In their place I would probably have lost my nerve, I admit. Although they didn't make a very relaxed impression, they didn't give up. They fought on.

"DOCTOR, DOCTOR!" Enrico croaked in a quavering voice. He sounded immensely old — ninety at least. "You've got to help me, doctor!"

"Now, now, my good man," said Caruso, playing a gentle, kindly doctor. "What seems to be the trouble?"

"I'm a circus artiste," quavered Enrico. "My trick is to walk on my forepaws and eat a carrot at the same time, but now I'm ninety years old."

"I see. . . . And now you can't walk on your forepaws anymore?"

228

"Oh yes, doctor, I can do that all right."

"Really? So what's the problem?"

"It's the carrots, doctor. I can't chew them anymore, not now. I've lost all my teeth."

OH DEAR, OF DEAR, OH DEAR . . .

Goldoni was sitting there with a face like stone.

All at once he started to shake.

And then he emitted a loud, raucous peal of laughter. He laughed and laughed and laughed. "Walking on his forepaws!" he gasped. "Carrots! No teeth!" He sat back in his chair and threw up his hands. "By all the saints," he guffawed, "was that droll!"

Suddenly he stopped laughing.

His arms went limp, his head sagged sideways, and his eyes glazed over.

"Your Excellency!" cried Francis. "What's the matter?" He turned to Yakoub. "Is he . . . dead?"

"No, he has simply lost consciousness," the hakim replied. "If you want to save him, Brother Francis, untie me."

The monk hesitated. "First you must give me your word not to —"

"Untie me!" Yakoub shouted.

"Of course, Hakim, at once." Francis took the dagger from the table and cut his bonds.

"He must lie flat," said Yakoub. "You take his ankles!"

They carried Goldoni over to his cot. "And now release my daughter."

Francis hesitated again.

"BE QUICK!"

Francis severed Atira's bonds as well.

"Dearest Father," she said, "I can explain everything."

"There's no need, my turtledove." Yakoub smiled down at her. "I can put two and two together, and besides, I must save the knight's life first. If he dies, things won't look good for us." He opened one of the pouches on his belt. "Meanwhile, you can attend to those two courageous animals." He pointed to the table.

Enrico and Caruso were

230

lying flat on their tummies and had closed their eyes — they were recuperating. Yakoub produced a slice of melon from his pouch. "I suspect they like this sort of thing. It'll fortify them."

Atira deposited the slice of melon in front of the guinea pigs, but they merely blinked at it and shut their eyes again. "Then have a rest first," Atira told them.

Meantime, from another pouch, the hakim had produced a small flask containing liquid of some kind. He trickled a few drops of it between Goldoni's lips.

That was when I remembered why we were there.

We had traveled back in time to obtain something from the knight's person, and Yakoub could help us to do this. He had only to snip off a hair or two. "Sir William," I whispered, "WE CAME HERE TO—"

"— obtain something from Goldoni's body, I know," Sir William whispered back. "The only question is, can we afford to leave our hiding place? Tjark, my friend, what do you think?"

"The odds on our tangling with the monk are seventy-five to one," Tjark said in a low voice. "In view of the fact that it's getting light . . ."

It was indeed. The light of dawn was streaming through the crack between the tent flaps.

". . . I suggest we adopt the following course of action." Tjark broke off. Goldoni had uttered a groan and opened his eyes.

"The odds now stand at ninety-five to one," Tjark announced. "I suggest we do nothing for the present. I'll carry out an analysis of the new situation."

The first aspect of the new situation was that the knight sat up and jerked his head at the flask in Yakoub's hand. "What's that?" he demanded.

"The potion that brought you back to life. And now lie down again."

"What then?"

"Then I'll set my assistants to work on your wound."

"Your assistants?"

"They'll cleanse it. A week from now you'll be cured."

"Only a week?" Goldoni sank back against the pillows. "Who are these miracle workers of yours?"

Yakoub had opened a third pouch and taken out a glass tube with a cork stopper. "My miracle workers?" He removed the cork. "They're maggots."

"**MAGGOTS?!**" Goldoni sat up again, but Yakoub forced him back. "You wish to be rid of the pain?"

Goldoni nodded.

"Then trust me. You're suffering from gangrene. The flesh around the wound is putrefying. These bluebottle maggots will consume the rotten flesh and allow the wound to heal. They don't touch healthy tissue."

"I don't know why you're doing this for me." The knight raised his head and looked at Yakoub. "But

233

you're wrong if you think I'll release you in exchange."

"I don't think anything of the kind, but how would it have benefited me to let you die? Now lie still."

Goldoni sank back against the pillows once more and closed his eyes.

Carefully tapping the glass tube with his forefinger, Yakoub emptied some maggots onto the knight's wound. The creatures must have been pretty small, because I couldn't see them. "They're roughly the size of grains of rice," Tjark reported. I'd always thought he had better eyesight than befitted a hamster.

"Go to work, my friends," said Yakoub.

And the maggots proceeded to munch away.

I couldn't hear them munching, of course. Even a hamster's ears aren't as

234

sensitive as that, but it was obvious from the way Yakoub bent over the wound, closely observing what was in progress there, that the maggots were filling their bellies with the knight's rotting flesh.

Yakoub draped a cloth over the wound. "You're going to lie there without moving today, do you hear? **LIE STILL.** Tomorrow I'll make you a dressing, and a week from now we'll see what my assistants have accomplished." He straightened up. The knight lay there with his eyes closed.

Now was our chance to snip a few hairs from his head, but how could we convey this to Yakoub?

Brother Francis had stationed himself near the knight's cot and was following the proceedings with a suspicious eye. He would raise the alarm at once if he overheard us. If that happened, we could not, unfortunately, assume that Goldoni would continue to obey doctor's orders and lie still.

"Francis," the knight asked suddenly, "where are those funny little animals?"

235

"On the table, Your Excellency."

"Make sure they don't escape. You'd better shut them up in the chest again."

"At once, Excellency." Francis turned and made for the table.

Atira was standing beside Enrico and Caruso, who had woken up and were wide-eyed with fear.

Do something, Atira! **DO SOMETHING!**
Once they're back in the chest, we'll never be able to —

She looked at her father inquiringly, but he gave a little shake of the head. "Don't anger the knight," his expression conveyed. "We'll wait for another opportunity."

But what if they didn't get one?

Francis was now at the table. He reached for Enrico and Caruso with both hands, then stopped short. He raised his head and listened.

A hubbub had broken out in the camp.

"They're all shouting at once," Tjark whispered. "The words are hard to distinguish. . . . just a moment . . ." He listened. Suddenly he said, "There! Now I've got it."

And he translated:

"THE SHIPS ARE COMING! OUR SHIPS FROM HOME ARE COMING!"

CHAPTER FIFTEEN

"THE SHIPS ARE COMING, EXCELLENCY!" Brother Francis shouted. "Our ships from home are coming, just as I predicted!" He dashed to the mouth of the tent, wrenched open the lacing and thrust the flaps aside. Dazzling daylight streamed in. Francis ran off.

Cavaliere Goldoni had sat up and was listening. The cloth had fallen from his forehead to the ground. "The ships, by thunder!" He ran a hand over his wound, brushing off the maggots that clung to it, and sprang to his feet. "Honor and renown, bloodshed and adventure!" he cried, and hurried after Francis.

Atira and her father stood staring at the mouth of the tent in silence. Then Yakoub looked at the cloth lying on the ground. "He truly is past saving," he said, shaking his head.

That was when I had a

FLASH OF INSPIRATION. . . .

I darted out from under the chest and over to where the cloth had landed. And there they were.

Whitish, no bigger than grains of rice, and wriggling, they were maggots with Cavaliere Goldoni's flesh in their innards.

"Freddy," cried Atira, "where have you been?"

But I couldn't answer right away.

I WAS BUSY.

I was collecting the maggots in my cheek pouches, the receptacles nature has provided us with. They're absolutely dry (no hamster wants to store damp grain in his larder), so the dear little creatures wouldn't be damaged by saliva.

Tjark had also emerged from under the chest. "We were never very far from you, mistress," he said.

Sir William sprang onto the table. "You acquitted yourselves magnificently, boys," he told the guinea pigs.

"BRAVO, BRAVISSIMO!"

239

Enrico and Caruso raised their heads. "Please don't, Sir William," Enrico pleaded. "We can't endure the sound of applause."

"Still less the sound of critical remarks," groaned Caruso. "Never again for as long as we live."

"Understandable, quite understandable. But now we must get you down off this table. Atira, would you be so kind?"

Atira nodded. She picked up Enrico and Caruso and deposited them on the floor. Tjark came running over and the guinea pigs got to their feet. They seemed to be perking up already.

"Hi, you two," said Tjark. "That was cool, honestly. I wouldn't have managed it myself, I'd have ended up in the cooking pot."

Enrico and Caruso grinned. "You know what would have happened then?" Enrico asked.

Tjark shook his head. "Tell me."

"Goldoni would have cracked a tooth on you," said

Caruso. "No amount of stewing would ever soften *you* up, my plastic pal."

Tjark doubled up with a fit of the giggles.

Sir William jumped down off the table and joined the trio, and I came over to them.

"Well, Freddy," said Hakim Yakoub, "did they taste good?"

I merely nodded. I could never have explained to him why I needed the maggots.

"Brilliant idea, old boy," Sir William told me approvingly. "A sample of the knight's flesh, eh? THAT COMPLETES OUR MISSION."

Tjark made no comment. Suddenly he said, "There's something wrong with the maggots."

"Why? You think rotting flesh will be no use to Signor Goldoni?"

"No, it isn't that, it's something else. Signor Goldoni said something once. . . . **WHAT ON EARTH WAS IT?**" Tjark searched his data bank, then shook his head. "I can't place it," he said unhappily.

"Never mind," Sir William said consolingly, "I'm sure you'll think of it sooner or later." He cocked his head and listened. "The camp is still in turmoil, no one will pay any attention to us. I think we should say good-bye to Yakoub and Atira and make good our escape."

Meanwhile, Yakoub had taken his daughter in his arms. "Dearest Father," Atira was saying, "you aren't angry with me, are you?"

He wagged his head. "A trifle angry, my turtledove, because it was quite a shock when Durdana told me you weren't in your bedroom. But it quickly occurred to me that you must have sneaked off to the camp with the animals through the drain hole in the cellar."

"You knew about it? I mean, you knew one could crawl through it and emerge outside the walls?"

Yakoub nodded. "I've known it since I was a boy."

"Did you ever crawl out that way?"

"No," Yakoub replied sadly. "*I* didn't, my playmates did. I was too big and fat, even then."

"Worthy Hakim Yakoub," began Sir William, translated by Tjark. "Permit us to express our most sincere —" He broke off to listen. "The knight and the monk," he gasped, "they're coming back! **TAKE COVER!**"

We dove into our hiding places beneath and behind the chest just as the two men entered the tent.

"Very sensible of you not to try to escape," Goldoni said to Yakoub. "You wouldn't have gotten far. Do you know what has happened?"

"Presumably, the thing we city dwellers were afraid of."

"And the thing we Crusaders were hoping for. Our fleet, which has catapults onboard, is now blockading the harbor entrance. From now on, this will be a siege worthy of the name. It will end in the capture of Sidon."

"That remains to be seen." Yakoub was standing, tall and erect, in the middle of the tent. "We shall put up a resolute defense."

Goldoni nodded. "Of that I'm sure. It will be a fierce but honorable fight."

"Which the unbelievers are bound to lose," Brother Francis put in. "Why? Because the true faith always prevails. I proclaim that incontrovertible truth, Your Excellency, in my capacity as a man of God."

"Is that so, little monk?" Goldoni smiled sarcastically. "In any event," he went on, turning to Yakoub, "my thanks for your trouble. In view of the new situation, my wound

244

has ceased to matter either way. I grant you and your daughter safe-conduct back to the city. Two soldiers will escort you to the gates. More than that I cannot do for you, so farewell. Come, Francis."

He went to the mouth of the tent and paused there. Addressing thin air, he said, "If you're still in here, funny little animals, you did well. You're two genuine comedians." So saying, he went out with Francis following at his heels.

"Well, little monk," we heard him say outside the tent, "fetch two soldiers to act as escorts."

"Why me, Your Excellency? In any case, it's over. Being a man of God, I refuse to act as your errand boy any longer. Now that the Almighty has fulfilled my prophecy, it's certain that I shall be made a saint after my death."

"Unless you obey my order forthwith, little monk,

YOU MAY BE SAINTED SOONER THAN YOU LIKE!"

"Very well, Excellency, but this is the last time." The monk's voice grew fainter. "And don't expect me to

245

interpret for you again. I won't recite plays performed by animals of any kind, not anymore."

Goldoni said bitingly, in the distance, "You will, little monk. If I command you to do so, you will. In any case, what else will you do with that gift of yours?"

"I shall preach the word of God to animals. . . ."

Silence.

We emerged from our hiding places.

"Well," said Yakoub, "it's time to say good-bye."

Sir William drew himself up. "Worthy Hakim," he said, "we thank you and wish you the best of good fortune. Atira, you deserve our special thanks. Had it not been for you —"

"TEN MINUTES, NINETEEN SECONDS,"

Tjark broke in.

"Are you crazy?" I glared at him. "What happened to the rest of your energy?"

He shrugged. "No idea. It was the stress, I suppose. The excitement. The fear."

"Fear? You, an electronic hamster, were afraid?"

Tjark nodded. "Not at first, but in the end. I didn't realize I was a system capable of registering emotions." He paused. "Let me put it this way," he continued. "Earlier on, when Enrico and Caruso were playacting for their lives, it really broke me up." He thought for a while, then he said, "When my energy runs out, it'll mean I'm dead, won't it?"

HE WaS MORTaLLY aFRaiD—

he was scared of dying. I cleared my throat. "Look, Tjark, that really isn't the point at issue now."

After a moment's silence, Tjark said, "Anyhow, there's no way I can make it back to the bush under my own power."

"No problem," said Sir William. "I'll carry you, my friend."

"I suggest you take Freddy first. But please be as quick as you can. If we don't take off soon, I won't have enough energy left for the return trip."

Or for his personal survival, I thought.

247

"Up you get, Freddy!" called Sir William, and I climbed on.

"Where are you two off to?" Atira asked. Her scent of jasmine suddenly hit me again. Strange that I'd been unaware of it all this time.

I caught a last glimpse of her standing there, a short, slender figure with a turban and a blackened face.

And a last glimpse of Yakoub, the giant with the massive beard.

"We must all leave you soon, mistress," I heard Tjark say as Sir William bore me off.

The Crusaders' camp was deserted. The whole of the

besieging army had gone off to welcome the fleet, it seemed, so Sir William was able to take the direct route to our bush.

Some half dozen ships with red crosses on their sails were lying offshore, as far as I could make out, and another had dropped anchor right in front of the harbor mouth. Sidon was effectively cut off from the outside world. What would happen when the Crusaders captured the city? What would they do to its inhabitants?

Once beneath the bush, I slid off Sir William's back. "Won't be long," he said hurriedly, and sprinted off again.

I looked around.

Where was Zuleika?

"ZULEiKA! ZULEiKA!"

No reply.

She wasn't there. For some reason, she hadn't waited for me. . . .

I would have to leave here without being able to say good-bye to her. . . .

"ZULEiKA?"

Nothing.

Should I look in her burrow? But what if the others appeared in the meantime? Then every second might count. If Tjark didn't leave in time — if he didn't have enough juice left for the return journey — he would die.

And someone else would die too.

Goldoni's son would succumb to his blood disease because I hadn't returned with Cavaliere Goldoni's DNA. . . . The maggots were tickling my cheek pouches. . . . I *had* to go back.

Without having seen Zuleika one last time?

"Freddy!"

"ZULEiKA!"

She came toward me with a beaming smile. "Thank heavens! I was so worried about you."

She'd been worried about me!

"There was a sudden hubbub in the Crusaders' camp," she said. "A big commotion, I didn't know why. I thought it might have something to do with the hakim and his daughter. And so with you. I was afraid something had happened to you." She sat down in front of me. "I nearly went crazy. I ran off to my burrow, hoping that Nazira was there and had brought some news, but of course she wasn't. She never is in the mornings." Zuleika sighed. "But now everything's all right."

"ZULEiKA," I said, "my friends will be here in a minute. And then . . ." I broke off. I simply couldn't go on.

She nodded. "I know you all have an important mission to fulfill, you told me so." She gazed at me earnestly. "But don't forget: A hamster without a burrow is like a plant without roots." She came nearer. "The ground here is very suitable."

I shut my eyes and inhaled her fragrance.

The next moment, I felt her whiskers brush mine.

After a while she detached herself from me and I opened my eyes again. She was still very near.

"GOOD-BYE, FREDDY."

"ZULEIKA . . ." My voice failed me.

She turned away and walked to the edge of the bush, where she paused and looked back. She smiled her enchanting, slightly lopsided smile. "We'd make good neighbors, Freddy."

And she disappeared into the undergrowth.

The pain of parting . . . I'd never realized that it was an actual pain, like a hand squeezing your heart.

But I had no choice. I could feel the maggots squirming in my cheek pouches. . . .

Just then Sir William reappeared, followed by Enrico and Caruso. Tjark slid off Sir William's back, looking thoroughly harassed.

"Quickly, quickly!" Tjark gasped. "There are only seconds left. Take up your positions! Quickly, please!"

We adopted exactly the same formation as we had on the outward journey: Tjark between Enrico and Caruso with Sir William and me facing them.

"**TEN** . . ." Tjark was starting the countdown. "**NINE** . . ."

The maggots were tickling my cheek pouches.

"**EIGHT** . . ."

Just a minute! They were tickling me. . . . The maggots were alive. . . .

"**SEVEN** . . ."

They were creatures from this medieval world. . . .

"**SIX** . . ."

The maggots didn't come from our world. They didn't come from the future. . . .

"FIVE . . ."

And Goldoni had said . . . *That* was what Tjark had failed to recall. . . .

"FOUR . . ."

" 'You can't visit the future unless you come from there. . . .' "

"THREE . . ."

So the maggots wouldn't *arrive* in the future.

"TWO . . ."

When *we* got there, *they* would have ceased to exist. . . .

"ONE . . ."

Our mission had failed.

"ZERO!"

CHAPTER SIXTEEN

DID I MENTION THAT, WHEN WE ARRIVED IN SYRIA, I was overcome by a feeling of nausea more intense than any I'd ever experienced before?

That was true and remained so — but only until we got back from Syria, because what now afflicted me was the nausea of nauseas, the mother of all queasiness. I didn't even feel like vomiting, just as if every last cell in my body was putrid and disintegrating.

Sir William was puking up his guts beside me. Enrico and Caruso, too, had fared badly this time. Very badly, in fact. They were moaning and whimpering like — well, like a pair of guinea pigs on the point of being slaughtered.

Tjark was lying flat on his stomach with his eyes closed, utterly motionless. He had obviously used up his very last milliwatt of energy.

I seemed to see all this through a sheet of ground glass. I was as incapable of rational thought as a runny, overripe

Camembert cheese. And, unlike my earlier bout of nausea, this one promised to be pretty long-lasting.

In a kind of trance, I registered the fact that the inner sphere of the time machine, our point of arrival, was gliding downward, that the hatch opened, and we were lifted out. I heard a murmur of voices among which the words "Thank heavens!" glimmered briefly like a light in darkness. Then I passed out.

When I recovered consciousness, I knew even before I opened my eyes that it was over. I felt as chipper as a hamster emerging from hibernation in springtime. But only physically. As yet, nothing much was happening in my head.

"HELLO, KID," I heard Mr. John say. I opened my eyes to find myself lying on the table in Goldoni's laboratory, the one with the laptop on it. Mr. John was smiling down at me. Linda, wearing her apple-and-peach-blossom perfume as usual, was standing across from him. She beamed at me and nodded. Lying on the table not far away were Sir William and the guinea pigs.

All three still had their eyes shut. Where was Tjark? Where, for that matter, was Goldoni?

"Signor Goldoni is just refueling Tjark," Mr. John said. "He plugged him into an external power source as soon as you landed, so that he could submit a preliminary report."

Mr. John paused.

"Goldoni took the news calmly."

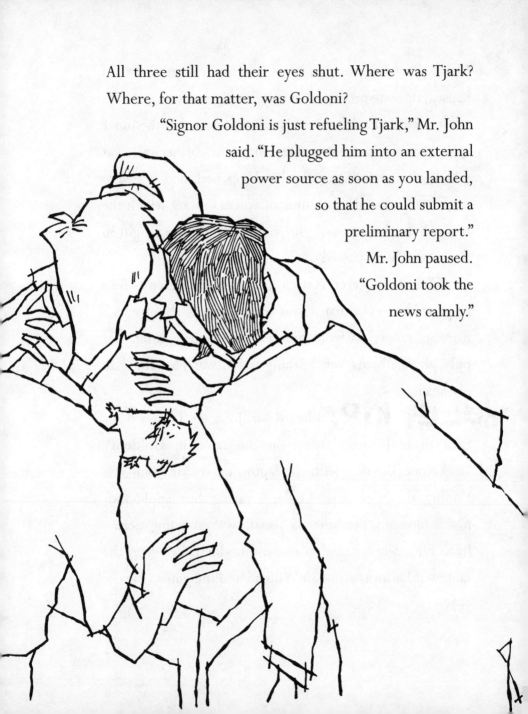

"He was rather disappointed, of course," Linda added.

Disappointed? About what? I struggled to get my gray cells working.

At that moment Goldoni appeared. "*Bene*, I'm glad you're feeling better," he said. "Tjark simply hadn't enough energy left to power your physical functions."

His big black mustache was drooping mournfully. "Freddy, *caro mio*, you acted with great presence of mind. I can't thank you enough."

So I'd displayed great presence of mind, had I? Naturally, I always did, but what was he talking about?

"The only trouble was," Goldoni went on sadly, "it didn't work — it couldn't."

What couldn't?

"Traveling into the future is impossible. Only animals that have *come* from the future can do that, and those little creatures hail from the twelfth century."

These little creatures? The maggots! He was talking about the maggots. . . .

They weren't tickling me anymore.

259

Goldoni was right.

On the other hand, there was something inside my cheek pouches. . . . **THEORETICALLY.**

I ran both paws over my cheeks to empty the pouches and ejected their contents onto the table.

And there they were. The maggots!

Not one of them was squirming. They were all dead.

Goldoni stared down at them. "The maggots," he said. "The maggots containing my ancestor's flesh. My ancestor's flesh . . . But . . . how can that be?" He went on staring.

Suddenly he smote his forehead. "But of course! That's it! *Precisamente!*" A broad smile appeared on his face. "I thought that anyone who tried to travel into a future from which he hadn't come would vanish without trace into the space-time continuum. But it isn't like that. You simply arrive in the future dead.

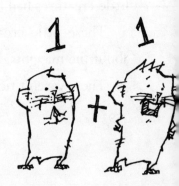

Bene, bene, bene!" He nodded to himself. "Freddy, *caro mio*, I shall dedicate this discovery to you. How would

FREDDY'S FIRST LAW OF TIME TRAVEL'

suit you?"

I raised both paws. No objection. Very flattering and gratifying. Theoretically.

Except that it wasn't all that important to me, not now.

All five of us animals were back in Mr. John's apartment.

All *five*? Yes, because Tjark was now one of the family. He'd been living with us for the last three weeks, and

from now on he would continue to do so on a permanent basis. This had been decided at a meeting of the family council.

"I really meant to destroy the time machines once they had served their purpose," Goldoni had told us. "I will, too, but only the big machine in the factory. What about Tjark?" He paused and looked at us all. "I thought so," he said, "and I may tell you that it's Tjark's own dearest wish to live with you from now on." After that, the family council's decision was just a formality, as the saying goes.

As soon as he could find the time, Goldoni intended to dismantle the big machine, which was still capable of making a journey into the past. For the moment, however, he was too busy developing a cure for his son's genetic disease. "Another three months," he'd told us, "and I'll have done it."

I myself had plenty of plans in mind for the period after our return.

First, I had a score to settle with Enrico and Caruso.

That "medieval" skit of theirs had poked fun at my love for Sophie. I'd intended to punish the pair by flattening them. Then it transpired that they'd been expecting me to do so. "You mean you've known it all along?" I'd asked, and got no answer. I was now determined to extract one from them.

Because this was a matter that concerned the three of us alone, I waited until Mr. John had summoned Tjark to the kitchen to top up his energy supply. Goldoni had installed an apparatus there from which Tjark could draw fuel — hydrogen, to be more precise.

Enrico and Caruso had talked Linda into painting them a sign and hung it up above the entrance to their cage:

Laugh your way back to health with the tittersome trio! If of pain you've had your fill, our merry skits cure any ill. Recommended by medieval knights!

"Tjark's addition to our team has opened up a host of new opportunities," Enrico declared.

"Human audiences!" cried Caruso.

"Television engagements!" Enrico enthused.

"Guest appearances on talk shows!" Caruso said eagerly.

"I can already see the headlines," raved Enrico. "THE TITTERSOME TRIO COMEDY SERIES TOPS THE RATINGS!"

"If I remember correctly," I said, "it isn't long since two guinea pigs put the following statement on record:

264

'We can't endure the sound of applause, still less the sound of critical remarks. Never again for as long as we live.' Or am I mistaken?"

"Haven't you ever heard of stand-up comics?" Enrico demanded. "No?"

"Then look at us," said Caruso. "There are a couple of them standing up right in front of you."

Stand-up comics? That's my cue, you guys. I still owe you something for that tip you gave to "timid hamsters everywhere" — that advice to "let rip." That was just what *this* far-from-timid hamster was going to do right now:

LET IT RIP WITH A VENGEANCE!

I rose on my haunches and assumed my combat stance, fur bristling and cheeks inflated, let out a terrifying snarl, and . . .

And nothing.

They continued to stand there.

Enrico and Caruso had *not* toppled over backward. Those guinea-piggish comedians were *not* lying flat on their backs like a pair of helpless, upended dung beetles.

265

I came down on all fours again, feeling pretty mortified. I had to face the truth, distasteful though it was. "So you always knew when I was going to flatten you," I said.

"Do you mean," Enrico asked, "that we were playacting every time?"

"Or," Caruso put in, "in plain guinea-piggish, that we bamboozled you?"

That hit the nail on the head.

I nodded.

"**WE FOOLED HiM!**" cried Enrico.

"**WE FOOLED HiM!**" yelled Caruso.

"We *never* knew beforehand!" cried Enrico.

"We were *always* scared to death!" yelled Caruso.

"B-but . . ." I stammered. "You didn't fall over just now."

The guinea pigs glanced at each other.

"Shall we let him into our little secret?" asked Enrico.

"Yes, let's," said Caruso, "or he'll beat his brains to jelly."

"And that would be a shame."

"Because our Freddy isn't such a bad sort — for a hamster."

"You'll make me weep in a minute," I said. "Well, do I get to hear your secret or don't I?"

Enrico grinned. "Okay, here it comes. That time we performed our medieval skit, here in the cage . . ."

"Which we still think is the tops," Caruso chimed in, "even if Cavaliere Goldoni wasn't too taken with it."

"But he'd probably had an argument with his wife just before leaving for Syria," said Enrico, "and was afraid she might be —"

"The secret," I snapped. **"COME ON, OUT WITH IT."**

"Okay, okay." Enrico raised both paws in a soothing gesture. "Do you remember what Mr. John was doing just before we performed our skit?"

"Of course. He was translating my second book, *Freddy in Peril*."

Caruso nodded. "Can you remember where he'd gotten to?"

Where he'd gotten to? But of course! It was the bit where I'd bowled them over. So that was the solution to the mystery! Before he translated a sentence, Mr. John made a practice of reading it aloud to himself in a low voice.

"Once we'd overheard that, your combat stance ceased to scare us. We'll never fall over in a panic again."

"Sorry, Freddy, that little ploy has had its day. You can't use it to torment us anymore."

"What about you two? I suppose you've never tormented *me*?"

"We have." Enrico grinned. "Pretty effectively, too, I admit."

"Know what, Freddy?" Caruso looked at me. "As far as tormenting goes, we ought to agree that we're even. Deal?"

I looked at the two of them sitting there with their beady little eyes darting to and fro — Enrico small and scrawny, with long, red-and-white fur, and Caruso, big and plump with a short black coat flecked with white — I looked at them sitting there in front of me as they'd so often sat before, and said, "Okay, you guys. Deal."

HEIGH-HO . . .

Thus ended our legendary duel.

It was a bit of a shame.

More than a bit, in fact.

I was really going to miss it.

CHAPTER SEVENTEEN

I HAD "REQUESTED AN INTERVIEW" WITH SIR William. It was dumb of me to have put it in such highfalutin language, because His Lordship chose to receive me on his blanket in Mr. John's bedroom (Sir William is the only one of us privileged to sleep there). There he sat, a huge black tomcat, and only my innate self-confidence prevented me from feeling like a cockroach granted an audience with the Pope.

"Well, my friend, what's biting you?"

Aside from the fact that I never have fleas, what gave him the idea that I would come to him with my problems? "Nothing's biting me, Sir William. I simply, er, wanted to thank you."

"You wanted to thank me?" Sir William looked astonished. "What for, old boy?"

Hmm. That did present me with a problem after all.

Stupidly I hadn't thought it out beforehand. How was I to explain to Sir William why I was grateful to him?

Should I say: "Sir William, I'm grateful to you for not giving in to your predatorial instincts and gobbling me up the first time we met"? No, being a civilized, domesticated animal who has his instincts firmly under control, he would be offended.

Or should I say: "Sir William, thank you for finding solutions to so many of my problems, even though you aren't the brightest star in the sky"? No, that probably wouldn't please him either.

Or how about . . .

"Well, my dear fellow, what was it you wanted to thank me for?"

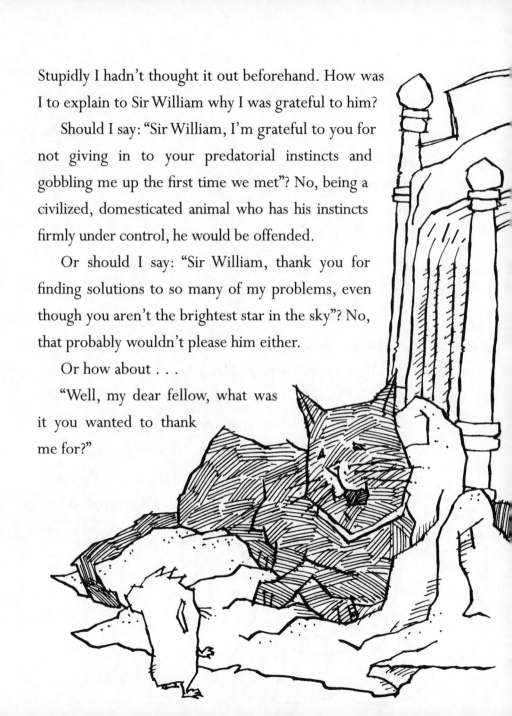

On the spur of the moment, I said, "For carrying me on your back so often and so readily."

Sir William looked at me. Then he slowly nodded his great head. "I see," he said. "Unless I'm much mistaken, however, there's more in your words of thanks than meets the eye."

Sir William — I want to state this for the record one more time — is what is known as a wise old tomcat.

"But while we're on the subject, my dear Freddy," he went on, "I'd like to thank you in return."

He wanted to thank *me*?

"Your arrival here at Mr. John's signaled a turning point in my life. I was well on the way to becoming a fat, lazy household pet. And what happened? We plunged headlong into that adventure with Professor Fleischkopf. It was immensely stimulating!"

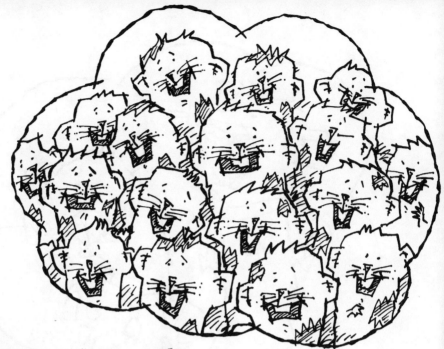

STIMULATING, EH?

I wouldn't have put it quite like that, not from my own point of view.

"And then came our adventure with those field hamsters we rescued. We've earned ourselves a place in the annals of wildlife conservation!"

Okay, but that hadn't been my real reason for going to such lengths.

"Next came the ferocious ferrets — a horrific episode. It made me feel years younger!"

You're welcome, Your Lordship. With the minor reservation that I almost bought the farm.

"And last of all a journey back in time to the Middle Ages. How many other tomcats can boast of such an experience?" Sir William inclined his head slightly. "Thank you, Freddy."

"Don't mention it," I said. "It was a pleasure."

Sir William's face took on a rather pensive expression. "One day, when I was sitting here on my blanket shortly after your arrival in this apartment, you told me you wanted to be a free-ranging domesticated animal."

Had I? As far as I could recall, I'd merely explained why I wanted to get in touch with Mr. John via his computer.

"I can tell you this now, my dear fellow: I never believed you'd do it."

"Never become a free-ranging domesticated animal, you mean? Why not?"

He eyed me thoughtfully. "It's obvious you've never given the matter any thought. But then," he said, nodding to himself, "it's only natural."

What was only natural? "Could you please express yourself a little more clearly?" I said, controlling myself with an effort.

275

"You're on the point of losing your temper again, aren't you?" Sir William grinned. "Have a smidgen of patience." He stretched out comfortably on his blanket. "It's like this, my friend. Certain animals have lived with humans for thousands of years — cows, pigs, and dogs, for example. Humans have bred those domesticated animals accordingly. Not just because they wanted more milk or meat or better watchdogs, but to make their communal existence work. Domesticated animals are less aggressive than wild animals and get along better with other species."

"But what's that got to do with me?" I demanded. "You didn't mention cats, incidentally. You're a domesticated cat yourself."

"True," said Sir William. "And there's another species of domesticated animal living here with us."

Another species? "Do you mean Enrico and Caruso, by any chance?"

"Exactly. They're no wilder than I am. The early inhabitants of Central and South America were breeding guinea pigs as household pets thousands of years ago." Sir William paused. "And now tell me, Freddy: **WHAT ARE YOU?**"

Hmm. I'd never given the matter any thought, it was true, perhaps because I wasn't too keen to know the truth. Humans had never bred our kind to be household pets, so the fact remained that I was a wild animal. Was I an aggressive creature that didn't get along with other animals? "Okay," I said. "But why do you think I manage to live here like a household pet with the run of the apartment? With you and Enrico and Caruso, I mean?" I paused, then added, "I'm not as aggressive as all *that*, am I?"

"Certainly not. You're quite bearable." Sir William grinned. "However, Freddy, you managed to fit into our family only because you found an outlet for your aggressive urges."

What did he mean? Jogging on my hamster carousel, or . . . ? "Oh you mean my, er, writing?"

Sir William nodded.

Authorship as a remedy for biting? **GREAT!**
Instead of sinking my teeth into Enrico and Caruso, I
pounded away at the keyboard with my paws. Well,
well . . . . What could I say? It was true, actually!
Many was the time I'd worked off my irritation
with the guinea pigs and Sir William by pouring it
out on the screen.

"And Enrico and Caruso?" I asked. "If they're such
peaceable domesticated animals, why do they need
those skits of theirs?"

"They could dispense with them anytime, old boy.
To them, those skits are just a joke. They're not

meant to be taken seriously, whereas you learned to read and write because you badly needed to do so."

He was right, no doubt about it. I thought for a moment. "What all this implies, Sir William, is that if I lived in the wild like the wild animal I am, I wouldn't need to write anymore." I paused. "In fact I probably wouldn't miss it too much."

"I'm quite convinced you wouldn't," Sir William said firmly. He paused, fixing me with his extraordinarily green eyes. Then he said, "Whatever you decide, you have my blessing."

His Lordship had, after all, managed to end our conversation like the Pope concluding an audience.

But I was happy to have spoken with him, indeed I was. Happy as a hamster that had just caught one of those nutritious and exceedingly tasty Syrian beetles.

"Thank you, Sir William," I said.

"THANK YOU FOR EVERYTHING."

Enrico and Caruso were fast asleep. Tjark was asleep, too, but not inside their cage with them. They weren't on such intimate terms. He was stretched out in front of the entrance — his temporary sleeping place, because soon he would be getting a regular hamster cage of his own.

"Tjark?" I whispered, and he was up in a flash. He hadn't been asleep, of course, just vegetating in his energy-saving mode. Thanks to some highly effective sensors, he could switch to full operation within milliseconds.

"Why are you whispering?" he whispered.

"I don't want to wake Enrico and Caruso. I'd like a word with you alone."

"Okay," he whispered, "then we'll take a stroll across the study." He had naturally surveyed every corner of the apartment and stored the relevant data, but why shouldn't he make use of his abilities?

"Tjark," I asked him, "can you read?"

"What for?" He grinned. "I already know all there is to know."

"So you can't write either."

"No, I don't have to. If I want something from Mr. John, I simply ask him."

Hmm. As far as the technical side of communicating with humans was concerned, Tjark was the perfect household pet.

"Listen," I said, "it's about Sophie. I'd have liked to introduce you to her, but she's still on vacation. She's someplace far away with her parents."

"SOPHIE? YOUR FORMER MISTRESS?"

"Exactly. She visits me regularly and she always brings me a mealworm. Perhaps you could pretend to . . . No?"

Tjark had shaken his head vigorously. "No, not again. I won't pretend to be someone I'm not."

"So what *will* you do?"

"I'll say: Mistress, I'm an electronic hamster. There are lots of things I can't do that a genuine hamster can, for instance, eat a mealworm. But I *can* do things a genuine hamster can't, for instance, talk with you. Sophie, my mistress, make up your mind whether or not you like me!"

Well, well. From the look of it, this electronic hamster possessed an endearing-himself-to-Sophie chip in addition to all the rest.

OKAY. HE HAD MY BLESSING.

It was around ten o'clock in the morning, and I was sitting at the keyboard of Mr. John's computer.

As usual, I was feeling as dozy as a human who'd crawled out of bed at three in the morning. A nocturnally active rodent like me should be in his nest by mid-morning, but it couldn't be helped. I would never get used to living in conflict with my internal clock, that had become quite clear to me. I wouldn't even get used to not getting used to it.

Tjark had returned to the guinea pigs' cage after our conversation and reverted to his energy-saving mode. The other members of the family had long been asleep in

any case, so it had been my lot, as so often, to spend the long night alone and wide awake.

On such a night, I would once upon a time have turned on the computer and continued writing a book. Or started a new one. That would really have been the thing to do, because I naturally wanted to make a story out of our experiences in Syria. But that night I simply couldn't.

I felt very lonely.

WRETCHEDLY LONELY.

I started to ponder. And then to brood. But I soon realized it was pointless brooding. I wouldn't come to a decision unless I consulted someone.

And that someone could only be Mr. John. But he was asleep.

So I'd vaulted onto my hamster carousel and proceeded to jog like crazy. Although that helped a bit where the brooding was concerned, it had been a long, long night. And a lonely one.

Now I was sitting at the keyboard of Mr. John's Mac, waiting for him.

He'd finished translating my book, *Freddy in Peril*, yesterday, so he was later than usual getting up today. However, I could already hear him clattering around in the kitchen. At last he came into the study with a mug of coffee in his hand.

"Morning, kid," he said, sitting down at his desk. "Been waiting for me?"

I nodded. *Good morning, Mr. John*, I typed. *I need your help.*

"Really?" He took a sip of coffee. "What's it about?"

I can't explain without going back a bit. Okay?

"Sure, fire away."

I thought for a moment. Then I typed: *It's about Assyria.*

"I see." He nodded. "You mean about the golden hamsters' paradise." He nodded again as if he'd been expecting me to raise the subject.

Up to now I knew about two Assyrias, I typed. *The Promised Land my great-grandmother described to me, and the one I found by learning to read and write.* I paused. Then I added, *Great-Grandmother's Assyria was just a fable. We can forget about it.*

"I think so too." Mr. John looked at the monitor. "You said: '*Up to now I knew about two Assyrias.*'" He turned to me. "Time travel introduced you to another Assyria, didn't it?"

I nodded.

"So now there are two Assyrias again," he said. "But

this time they're two you *can't* forget."

I nodded again.

Mr. John regarded me in silence. All at once he said, "And you don't know which Assyria to choose. To be more precise, you're scared of committing yourself."

I stared at him. How did he know that?

"You're wondering how I knew?" He smiled. "It wasn't hard to guess. You've changed, Freddy. You usually start work as soon as you get back from one of your adventures. But this time? You haven't written a word since you returned, and you've never been so restless."

Mr. John — I must state this, too, for the record — is the smartest human being I know.

287

It's true, I typed. *I'm scared of making a decision. It's so terribly final. If I ever regret it, it'll be too late. I'll be stuck.*

"Hmm." Mr. John eyed the screen thoughtfully. "You know, of course, that I can't make up your mind for you. The decision is yours and yours alone, right?" When I nodded, he went on: "But I think I can help you all the same."

I sat up eagerly.

"I suspect you're looking at the matter from only one angle. You must get one thing straight: Goldoni is scared stiff that his invention may fall into the wrong hands. As soon as he's developed the cure for his son, he'll destroy the time machine — that's a surefire certainty. And then, as you say, you'll be stuck in twelfth-century Syria."

EXACTLY.

"But!" Mr. John raised his forefinger. "If you remain here, what then?"

What then . . . ? I slowly sat down again.

Then I'd also be stuck.

Stuck here. Here in the Assyria of reading and writing. Here in this apartment with all it entailed.

Mr. John was right. I really hadn't thought of that.

"Maybe this'll help a little too," he said. "You're bound to have some regrets whatever you decide. But you can weigh those regrets against one another and see which side the scales come down. Then you can make your choice."

I'm doing just that, Mr. John.

"One last thing: When you've decided, once for all, I think your regrets will vanish because you'll be heart and soul behind your decision. But first you'll have to make up your mind."

I already did, Mr. John.

QUITE SUDDENLY EVERYTHING HAD BECOME CRYSTAL CLEAR.

I couldn't understand how I had ever been in any doubt.

Mr. John, I typed, *I'm now going to write something on the screen. When the time comes, will you pass it on?*

He nodded, and I typed:

289

For Sophie

My time with you is at an end,
this world I must depart.
Although I'm leaving, you will be
forever in my heart.

Remember this, dear: But for you
I never would have found
the earthly paradise for which
you helped to lay the ground.

That paradise for me began
when I learned how to write,
so I will never you forget,
though I am out of sight.

EPILOGUE

Freddy's decision was final.

And I, Mr. John, accepted it. What choice did I have?

Now that I've read Freddy's account of his experiences in Syria, I know his decision was the right one.

While reading it, I also realized that Freddy's mind was already made up when he consulted me. He later confirmed this. "I promised Zuleika I would come back," he told me. "She'll be waiting for me."

Freddy didn't type this last book on my keyboard like his previous works. He dictated it to Tjark, who transmitted it to my computer by infrared. Why such a roundabout route?

Because Freddy was running out of time. "I must get back to Syria as soon as possible," he said. "That way, I can dig myself a burrow and lay in some stores before the winter rains begin." So he dictated the book in the course of several all-night sessions and fed it into one of Tjark's numerous data banks. In Interanimal, of course. I mention this only because, interestingly enough, that telepathic language seems far better suited to the rapid and concentrated transmission of information than any human idiom.

Freddy gave me permission to correct his text if I considered it necessary. I did not consider it necessary. He had produced an extremely vivid and readable book. (Incidental note: It's rather a shame that such a promising author will never be heard from again.)

Because time was running out, Freddy couldn't wait here until Sophie returned from her vacation. She is now back home, and seems — after mourning his disappearance for a few days — to have gotten over it quite well with the aid of Tjark, who has been dancing attendance on her in the most chivalrous way. Moreover, thanks to him, she can now converse with Enrico and Caruso, and she finds it great fun when the "Tittersome Trio" performs amusing skits for her (the guinea pigs and Tjark have recently been planning to open an animal theater for children).

Freddy's actual departure was a rather melancholy event. For me, at least, and also for Linda.

The animals, on the other hand, seemed to take it calmly — indeed, quite cheerfully. It had been agreed between them and

Freddy that they wouldn't accompany him to the time machine. He said good-bye to them in my apartment, and he did so in a cheerful, jocular way. That, at least, was my impression. He slapped Enrico and Caruso on the back, gave Tjark a playful nudge, and rested his paw on Sir William's in a final token of farewell.

Signor Goldoni had everything ready. The generators were already running, and the time machine, that huge shiny silver sphere, seemed to be vibrating expectantly.

I put Freddy down on the table beside the laptop, which was on.

"Freddy, caro mio," said Goldoni, "you realize you can't return to our world without Tjark's help, and Tjark won't be there?"

Freddy nodded.

"And that I'll have to dismantle the big time machine in the near future?"

Freddy nodded again, several times.

"Bene," said Goldoni. "There's more than enough energy available for you on your own. That means you won't feel nauseous on arrival." He pointed to the digital display on the console. "The machine has naturally stored all the data required for your journey. You'll land in exactly the same spot as before, but time will have passed just as it has in our own world."

Which meant that the Crusaders would probably be besieging Sidon even harder than before. But that would be happening in the world of humans — a world with which Freddy, once back in Syria, would have no connection.

I had taken it for granted that he would bid us farewell with one of his famous waves, but he didn't. He typed on the laptop: Good-bye, Linda, and please don't change your perfume, okay?

"Okay," Linda said with tears in her eyes.

Then Freddy turned to me.

Thank you, Mr. John, for allowing me to live with you.

"You're welcome, kid."

I carried Freddy to the hatchway and placed him in it. Goldoni pressed a button and the hatch closed.

That was when sadness almost got the better of me.

Goldoni went over and stood behind the console. "Shall I?" he asked.

I nodded, and he operated a lever.

The hum of the generators grew louder, the shiny silver sphere's vibrations intensified, and columns of figures started racing over the display on the console.

Suddenly the display returned to zero.

Goldoni said, "He has landed."

You're there, Freddy.

Come out from under that bush and into the warm, balmy air. Revel in the silence, revel in the long-familiar scent of plants and flowers.

Scamper off to Zuleika's burrow and say hello to your pretty young neighbor.

Start digging a burrow of your own. Stock your larder with grain and pine kernels.

Be happy.

You've reached your Promised Land at last.

DIETLOF REICHE grew up in a family of five children. Over the years, the family adopted seven hamsters, but unfortunately, they eventually all ran away. Dietlof always wondered why they left and where they went. So he imagined Freddy, and there began the Golden Hamster Saga. Dietlof Reiche lives in Hamburg, Germany, with his wife.

JOHN BROWNJOHN has garnered many awards for his translations of more than one hundred books for children and adults, including the Helen and Kurt Wolff Prize, the U.S. PEN Prize, and the Christopher Award. He lives in Dorset, England.

JOE CEPEDA has created artwork for numerous book covers, magazines, and newspapers. He is also the illustrator of many award-winning picture books. He lives in California with his family.

BE SURE TO READ ALL OF FREDDY'S ADVENTURES!

I, FREDDY
BOOK ONE IN THE GOLDEN HAMSTER SAGA

FREDDY IN PERIL
BOOK TWO IN THE GOLDEN HAMSTER SAGA

FREDDY TO THE RESCUE
BOOK THREE IN THE GOLDEN HAMSTER SAGA

THE HAUNTING OF FREDDY
BOOK FOUR IN THE GOLDEN HAMSTER SAGA